Christmas with Sophie Sayers

Festive Tales from Wendlebury Barrow

Debbie Young

Hawkesbury Press

Dedication

To all who make Christmas music at St Mary's, Hawkesbury

Author's Note

Here is a special Christmas treat for all who have enjoyed the adventures of Sophie Sayers and friends in my series of mystery novels set in the little Cotswold village of Wendlebury Barrow. Some of the stories have appeared previously online, and one of them, *Christmas Ginger*, featured in LJ Ross's charity anthology, *Everyday Kindness*, to raise funds for housing charity Shelter. Others were written especially for this collection. All are inspired by the festive activities I enjoy in my own Cotswold village of Hawkesbury Upton.

The stories take place over several different Christmases, woven around the timelines of the growing series of Sophie Sayers novels. If you've read my Gemma Lamb mystery novels, set at St Bride's School in the same parish, you'll also spot familiar characters from those books in *The Secret Ministry of Frost*.

There are of course Christmassy novels in both series, (*Murder in the Manger* and *Sinister Secrets at St Bride's*), but these short stories are slightly different in tone: feel-good, upbeat fiction, with not a crime in sight. All are filled with the Christmas spirit and will leave you feeling festive.

Finally, some thank-yous: for the beautiful cover design and illustration by Rachel Lawston; the meticulous feedback from beta reader

Lucienne Boyce; and the polishing of the prose by editor Alison Jack. Last but not least, my thanks to the bell ringers and carol singers of my home village for the inspiration and joy they bring to my own Cotswold village Christmas.

With my very best wishes to you for a merry Christmas and a Happy New Year, this year, and every year.

Debbie Young

Hawkesbury Upton

Christmas 2023

The Vicar's
Christmas Letter

The Rectory, High Street, Wendlebury Barrow
1ˢᵗ December

D ear Nancy and Edward,

This year no doubt you were expecting to receive my annual Christmas letter from my little retirement cottage in the delightful Devonshire village of Appledore. To my surprise as much as yours, I write to you again from the parish of Wendlebury Barrow, where my successor, the Reverend Neep, sadly did not last long – through no fault of the parishioners, I hasten to add. I daresay your dear boy Hector regaled you with the details.

I confess I am not unhappy to have been recalled by the bishop to hold the fort until a permanent replacement may be found, and that the process is taking so long. Country pastors are so hard to come by these days. I cannot understand why. Life in Wendlebury Barrow is not without its challenges, but it is never dull, and the community is in the heart of the beautiful Cotswolds.

And so begins another Christmas. I'm looking forward to the delights of a traditional Cotswold festive season, from carols around the

Christmas tree on the village green to ringing in the New Year in our ancient bell tower, and everything in between.

Even though I was away on my supposed retirement for only a few months, new traditions have grown up in my absence. For example, we are to have a nativity play performed at St Bride's Church by the children of the village school and the Wendlebury Players. It's been written especially for our community by a newcomer, Sophie Sayers, who has experience in a travelling theatre company, Hector tells me. You will have known of Sophie at least by reputation before her move to the village, as your late friend May Sayers was her great-aunt.

I remember old May Sayers telling me not long before she passed away how our little community was a constant in her peripatetic life as a travel writer.

I believe Sophie has inherited her aunt's literary talents, although in a different guise. In her aunt's image, she has thrown herself into village life, having recently joined the choir. She is musical too, and has a charming singing voice, although, as you no doubt remember, our choirmaster values enthusiasm over accuracy, for the sake of swelling choir numbers.

I'm not surprised that she has charmed your Hector. Although some might counsel against mixing work with romance, as a local priest whose personal life and ministry cannot help but be intertwined, I'm inclined to approve.

I wonder when it will be his brother Horace's turn to settle down. Hector tells me his twin is unable to return from Australia this Christmas, but he will be in all our thoughts.

I trust your own retirement in Clevedon continues to bring you rest, peace and joy, and an abundance of all three in this season of goodwill.

I close with Christmas blessings to you both. If ever you would like a little holiday in Appledore, I know of the perfect cottage you are welcome to borrow, with my compliments, while I continue my ministry here in Wendlebury.

Yours truly,

Gerard

The Reverend Gerard Murray

A Not So Bleak Midwinter

'It doesn't feel the least bit like Christmas,' I complained to Hector as I added another couple of books to our window display of festive gift ideas. For most of the day, the sky had been a pure, clear forget-me-not blue, the air still, the sun beaming down fit to melt the fake snow on the inside of the glass.

'Just think of it as a green Christmas rather than a white one,' replied Hector, closing the door behind a customer heading off into the dusk. 'After all, we're giving a new lease of life to all that packaging material.'

Whenever either of us had a moment, we'd uncrumple the kraft paper that came wedged into our suppliers' boxes to stop books getting damaged in transit and iron it on the stockroom table. Then we cut it into A2 sheets to make it more manageable and put them at the centre of the children's play table in the bookshop's tearoom, alongside Christmas stencils and coloured felt-tip pens. Hey presto – environmentally friendly Christmas gift-wrap! Complimentary gift-wrapping of all books purchased in Advent encouraged locals to do their Christmas shopping at Hector's House rather than in town or online.

'That's child labour, that is,' declared Tommy, breezing in through the door as I stepped back from the shop window. Although local teenager Tommy is a regular visitor to the bookshop, he comes not for the books, but for the company. More often than not, he tries to blag a free milkshake. Occasionally, when flush from helping old Billy with odd jobs, he actually pays for one. We'd seen more of Tommy than usual this week, after their lucrative double-act hawking wheelbarrows of holly, ivy, and mistletoe around the village.

Tommy sat down on one of the child-sized chairs at the play table opposite his little sister Sina. His gangly legs ranged either side of the table like a young giraffe's.

'How much are they paying you to do that, Sina?'

He jabbed a grubby finger at her orderly rows of holly leaves. I thought he might put her off, but she was not so easily deterred, continuing to loop her green felt-tip pen along the edge of the stencil.

'Nothing, and I don't care, because it's fun. Actually, I think we're lucky Hector's not charging us to do it.'

Hector cleared his throat. 'And it's helping a good cause, Tommy. Two good causes, in fact: the environment, by finding a use for paper that would otherwise go for recycling, and the church.'

When Tommy looked dubious, I explained.

'Hector's donating the amount he'd usually spend on gift wrap to the church's Christmas charity appeal.'

'And very grateful we are too,' said the vicar, emerging from the non-fiction section with a couple of hardbacks. He set them down on the trade counter and took out his wallet to pay Hector. 'It's astonishing how many people forget to bring money for the Christmas service collections, or who find themselves short of cash once they've all finished their Christmas shopping. Priorities, my dears, priorities...'

While Hector gift-wrapped each book, the vicar took a seat at one of the tearoom tables.

'Cappuccino, please, Sophie. I think I've earned it after hosting the village school's visit to the church this afternoon.'

Sina laid down her green pen and beamed at the vicar.

'Yes, that was fun, especially getting a chocolate decoration each off the Christmas tree.'

Tommy pulled a sheet of paper towards him and picked up a black pen and a snowman stencil.

'You lucky duck! We never do anything like that at my school.'

Tommy had long since left the village primary school and now attended the nearest secondary school a few miles away.

'Chocolate wasn't the prime purpose of the visit,' said the vicar. 'I invited the children for a sneak preview of our crib.'

Each year, the vicar brings out an ancient set of china figurines to recreate the Bethlehem nativity scene. There's also a charming model stable, lovingly crafted in elm by some parishioner long since departed to the churchyard.

He's not daft, the vicar. Inviting the schoolchildren to view the crib is an effective way of enticing whole families to come to his Advent and Christmas services, persuaded by their children's delight in the traditional tableau.

Sina folded her arms.

'Yes, but it was a con, because the baby Jesus wasn't even there.'

Tommy drew a fierce expression on his first snowman, making it look like a chubby Halloween ghost. For a moment I thought he'd added two noses by mistake, then I realised they were fangs.

'Maybe today was the baby Jesus's day for playgroup.' Tommy glanced up to check Sina's reaction to his joke. Her expression was stern.

I hoped a young visitor hadn't pocketed the baby Jesus during the school visit. I could understand the temptation. There may have been no room for him at the inn, but he'd fit perfectly in a Sylvanian Family playhouse.

The vicar intervened.

'The thing is, Sina, Jesus isn't born until Christmas Day, so we don't add him to the crib till then. Come to the morning service on the twenty-fifth and you'll see him.'

I was ashamed to have forgotten that detail, despite having been a Sunday School teacher since Easter.

As I set the vicar's coffee on his table, Sina raised a forefinger to herald a bright idea.

'Why don't you just put his scan picture in the crib in the meantime? That's what people do who can't wait to see their real baby. My auntie had a scan picture of her baby in a frame on the mantlepiece for months before it was born.'

'Who's just been born?' asked Billy, entering the shop for the second time that day. 'Christmas babies always follow a good spring.'

'The baby Jesus,' replied Sina. 'Only he hasn't been born yet. That's the trouble.'

'You're two thousand years behind the times, girlie,' said Billy, touching his cap to the vicar. 'Don't that pesky internet teach you anything useful?'

'Coffee, Billy?' asked the vicar.

'That's very kind of you, vicar, but I'm here on a mission.'

'That should be your line, shouldn't it, vicar?' said Hector, as he opened the till and tipped a bag of pound coins into the cash drawer. 'What are you after, Billy?'

Billy untied his scarf. I was pleased to see he was wearing the one I'd made for him during the recent village craze for knitting.

'I'm after the right book for my old cousin Maurice.'

Hector had heard tales of Maurice before. 'You mean the one you haven't seen for twenty years?'

'Aye, that's the one.' He wagged a finger at Hector. 'You know I've been buying him a book here every Christmas, ever since you opened this shop of yours. So don't you go implying I'm neglecting him. I wouldn't do that, not with so few of my family left alive, God bless 'em.'

Like Tommy, Billy rarely buys a book, treating Hector's House like a social hub rather than a purveyor of fine reading materials. But that's okay. The best bookshops are much more than the means of buying a book – they are at the heart of the community. That's one of the reasons I love working here. Well, that and Hector. Soon after I started my job, Hector became my boyfriend as well as my boss.

Hector came out from behind the trade counter, rubbing his hands together.

'So, what's it to be this year, Billy? If I remember rightly, last year it was a collection of nature notes for every day of the year. Lovely woodcut illustrations, I recall.'

'Yes, and what a fine idea of yours that was. If Maurice has been using it properly, he'll have read a little bit each day and that'll have made him think of me all year round.' Billy lifted his cap to scratch his head. 'But I don't know about this year, Hector. What can I give him?'

'Poor as I am,' returned the vicar, quick as a flash. I smiled at the reference to Christina Rossetti's poem, "In the Bleak Midwinter", set to music by Gustav Holst. It's been my favourite Christmas carol since I learned it at primary school.

Hector consulted the non-fiction shelves for a few moments, then pulled out an astronomy guide with a map of the night sky for every week of the new year and an anthology of 365 poems.

'It must be hard to live at a distance from your relatives,' I said gently. My parents live in Inverness, hundreds of miles from our Cotswold village of Wendlebury Barrow, so I thought I knew how Billy must feel.

'Aye,' said Billy, taking the books from Hector to examine. 'Especially without a car. That's the only reason I regrets never learning to drive.'

The local bus company runs services as far as Slate Green, our nearest market town, but that's all. To travel further afield, you must change at Slate Green, and even then, you can't get beyond a radius of about ten miles.

'I don't want a heavy book, mind.' Billy weighed the two books up against each other, one in each hand. 'Postage ain't cheap these days.'

I was curious as to how far-flung Billy's relations were. I knew he'd lived in Wendlebury all his life, although his brother had left as a young man. I wondered whether he'd emigrated, like Hector's twin brother Horace.

'So where exactly does this Maurice live, Billy?' I asked. 'Is he still in the UK?'

Billy passed both books back to Hector with a shake of his head.

'Slate Green.'

The vicar slammed his coffee cup down on his saucer.

'What?' he and I cried together.

I fetched a cloth to wipe up the vicar's spillage.

'But you get the bus to Slate Green to go shopping at least once a week,' I pointed out. 'How come you've never found the time to call on him?'

Billy shuffled his feet.

'He ain't been to see me neither. It ain't my fault. Besides, we always used to meet at our mums' houses. His mum was my mum's sister. His mum or mine took turns to cook Sunday dinner and we'd all sit down together, both families. But them days are long gone, and so are our mothers. We was both so upset after they died, just a few weeks apart, that we never really got round to making new arrangements. We missed them too much, see. It just wouldn't have been the same without them.'

The vicar took the cloth from me to dry his saucer.

'That's a great pity, Billy. I've seen this happen far too often after a bereavement, just when you need your family most.'

Tommy looked up from his sheet of gift wrap. His latest row of snowmen had the threatening air of Mafia hitmen.

'Don't you like each other, then?'

Billy sat down opposite the vicar, his shoulders slumping.

'Bless you, no, boy, I've always liked him well enough. We was thick as thieves when we were your age. Always up to mischief in the village.'

'I wish I had a thief to be thick with.'

Poor Tommy. No other boys from his class lived in the village, one of the disadvantages of being raised in a small rural community.

'We had no end of make-believe games, neither – pirates, cowboys, Robin Hood.'

The vicar set down the cloth and reached across to rest his hand on the frayed cuff of Billy's ancient tweed jacket.

'Then I think this Christmas you should start making up for lost time. I'll run you down to see him any time you like. You have only to ask.'

Billy's face softened. 'Well, if Hector would just buck his ideas up about the right present...'

Suddenly Hector's face lit up.

'I know just the thing!'

And with that, he dashed out of the shop. The others looked puzzled at his unexpected departure, but when I heard Hector opening the front door to his flat at the side of the shop and running up two flights of stairs to his top floor, I knew what he was about.

Moments later, he reappeared in the shop doorway, breathless and triumphant, holding up a vintage hardback copy of *Treasure Island*. A colour plate on the cover showed a fierce-looking Long John Silver, complete with wooden leg, crutch, and parrot.

Billy's mouth fell open.

'Ah, now that's what I call a book.'

When Hector put it into his hands, he gazed at it with the rapture of a starving man reading a gourmet menu.

I came out from behind the tearoom counter to appeal to the children.

'Now, who wants to give Billy their paper to wrap his cousin's present in?'

To my surprise, Sina had laid aside her holly leaves unfinished, and was now scribbling in black pencil on a small square of plain white paper.

'I'm afraid it'll have to be Tommy's snowmen, Billy.'

Billy peered at Tommy's handiwork.

'They'll do very nicely, thank you, Tom.'

He took the paper to the trade counter for Hector to do the honours. When the vicar drained his coffee cup and got to his feet, I realised he was planning to drive Billy to see Maurice straight away before he could change his mind.

'Just a minute, vicar,' cried Sina, laying down her pencil and pushing back her chair. 'Here, I've made this for you. I know how much you're looking forward to Christmas and the baby Jesus and stuff, so here's something to keep you going.'

The vicar took the square of paper from her hand and turned it this way and that, narrowing his eyes.

'Ah, I see. It makes sense now I've spotted the halo.'

When he showed it to me, I too was at first puzzled by the array of fuzzy, broken lines, with just a dark kidney-shaped blob at the centre. Then it clicked.

'Oh yes, of course! Baby Jesus's scan photo! Well done, Sina. Very imaginative.'

Sina beamed and went back to colouring in her holly leaves, humming contentedly.

As the vicar escorted Billy, wrapped gift under his arm, out of the bookshop and into his car, I went to stand behind Hector at the trade counter, reading over his shoulder. He was logging Billy's purchase in the sales ledger he keeps for the second-hand book collection stored in his flat.

'You know what, Hector?' I said, draping my arms over his shoulders and clasping my hands on his chest. 'Suddenly it's starting to feel like Christmas after all.'

Hector closed the ledger and laid his hands gently over mine.

'So it is. Merry Christmas, sweetheart.'

The Secret
Ministry of Frost

'**C** old enough for you, Sophie Sayers?'

Billy banged the bookshop door behind him, stemming the icy blast that had heralded his arrival. Hector slapped one hand down on the trade counter just in time to stop a pile of bookmarks taking flight.

I smiled at my elderly friend as he plodded across to his favourite table in the tearoom.

'A bit of cold weather doesn't bother me. Spending my teenage years in the Scottish Highlands has set me in good stead for the worst a Cotswold winter can throw at me.'

When Hector winked at me, I could tell he was about to launch one of his 'wind Billy up and watch him go' conversation starters.

'Ah, but what about a Wendlebury winter?'

Billy took the bait.

'My old dad used to say, when it's jacket weather in Slate Green –' he was referring to our local market town down the hill '– it's overcoat weather in Wendlebury Barrow.'

Hector got up from his stool and strolled over to the tearoom counter to collect the coffee I'd just made for him. 'Or to put it more scientifically, living on top of the escarpment is colder than living below it.'

I wedged a mince pie onto Hector's saucer as he picked up his coffee before starting to prepare Billy's customary cappuccino.

'But nowhere in England gets as much snow as we do in the north of Scotland. In winter, there's often enough to make the main road to Inverness impassable. All along the road, there are poles at regular intervals, height marked so that you can see how deep the snow is at any point.' I paused while the milk steamer hissed. 'It's when you can't see the poles at all that you've got real problems.'

Billy unfurled the oatmeal scarf I'd knitted him, extracting its ends from deep inside the armholes of his jacket.

'You're too young to remember the long winter of 1963. The village was cut off for a fortnight. By the time the first tractor finally got through from Slate Green, our cupboards were bare.'

I sprinkled cocoa onto the top of Billy's coffee through a snowflake template.

'Of course, in them days, we still had several working dairy farmers in the village, so at least we had milk. The dairy lorries couldn't get through to collect it, and the farmers were glad to supply it to us rather than waste it. I thought we was going to end up like one of them roving tribes in Africa that I've seen on telly, who live off their cattle completely, drinking their blood as well as their milk.' He took a slurp of his coffee and smacked his lips in appreciation. 'What do you call them, Hector? Gnomes?'

'Nomads,' said Hector, suppressing a grin.

I cleaned the nozzle of the milk steamer with a cloth.

'So, what do you think of Carol's advice that it's too cold for snow?'

Carol Barker runs our village shop and is almost as full of dubious country lore as Billy.

Hector pursed his lips.

'It's not a question of temperature. It's just too dry for snow. Not enough water in the atmosphere, even though there's plenty under foot since that downpour a couple of days ago.'

Billy stirred the remains of the cocoa snowflake into his coffee.

'I just feels sorry for them young lads who'll have sledges for Christmas with no snow to slide 'em on.'

'And lasses too,' I put in, flicking the switch to make a drink for myself at last. I try to set Billy straight about equal opportunities when I can. His response showed how much effect I'm having.

'At least the girlies will like the pretty patterns left by Jack Frost.'

Hector took his coffee back to the trade counter, where a man was choosing a couple of book tokens from the display rack.

'But what about you, Sophie Sayers?' Billy enquired. 'If it's so snowy up by your folks, how will you get home to see them for Christmas? I don't suppose they'll want planes landing up there, slipping and sliding about the place, engines all frozen up.'

Hector gazed into the distance.

'I remember how upset your Auntie May was when she couldn't get up to Scotland to see you one snowy Christmas, a few years before she left this earth, God rest her soul. That Christmas ended well for her, though. I saw to that.'

I smiled in gratitude.

'Thanks for that, Hector. And don't worry about me, Billy.' I dropped a lemon and ginger teabag into my favourite cup and filled it from the kettle. 'I'm staying down south this year, spending Christmas Day and Boxing Day with Hector at his parents' house. Then we'll both fly into Inverness for Hogmanay.'

'What sort of hog is that?'

'You know, Hogmanay. The Scottish New Year. In Scotland, New Year is much more important than Christmas. They even have an extra public holiday on the second of January, to give them longer to get over it.'

Billy tutted.

'Drunken so-and-sos. But it looks like you two will have the best of both worlds, eh? The heart of their families is where everyone should spend their Christmas, and now you've got two families between you, lucky blighters. Since my cousin down in Slate Green died this summer, I ain't even got one.' He turned to Hector. 'I bet your old ma will be glad of the extra company, what with that brother of yours still being upside down.'

'My old ma, as you so unchivalrously call her, is at least fifteen years younger than you, Billy. And as I've told you before, despite being down under in Australia, Horace is as much the right way up as we are.'

Horace is Hector's identical twin, with the addition of the suntan and taut musculature that come from his job as a tour guide in the outback. He is as adventurous as Hector is reserved.

I pulled the pencil out of my ponytail and began doodling a koala in a Santa hat on my order pad.

'Hector, do you think Horace will have his Christmas dinner on the beach?'

Instead of answering, he got up to attend to a customer needing help in the languages section.

Billy grimaced.

'If you ask me, an Australian beach is a poor second to an English hearth and home.'

'So, what about you, Billy? Where will you have your Christmas dinner?'

I tried to think whether there were any other old people on their own in the village who might welcome Billy's company for Christmas dinner, but I drew a blank. Even Joshua, next door to me, so frail that he hardly leaves his house, was planning to go to his nephew's.

Billy wiped a speck of froth from his chin with the cuff of his tweed jacket before leaning back and clasping his hands across his tummy.

'Ah, well, I've decided to start my own tradition. The Bluebird is where I shall be filling my boots, beside Donald's roaring fire, kept warm at his expense, with no obligation to do the washing up. I hear Donald's missus does a lovely turkey roast with all the trimmings, plus Donald tells me you've never seen a pudden burn as bright as when he fires his up. Never skimps with the brandy.'

'Well, if a publican can't rustle up a good flambé, who can?' I doubted Hector would be as reckless with his favourite tipple on Christmas Day.

The shop phone trilled, and Hector returned to the counter to answer it.

'Mum, I've told you before, please don't ring me in the shop unless it's an emergency. It isn't an emergency, is it?'

His parents are at least ten years older than mine. They'd retired to the seaside town of Clevedon in Somerset a few years before, leaving Hector to turn their antiques shop into a bookstore. With Horace abroad, Hector feels solely responsible for their parents' welfare. As an only child myself, I understand.

Trying not to look as if I was eavesdropping, I emptied the dishwasher, arranging the clean cups, each branded with the name of a book and its author, on the old pine shelves behind the tearoom counter. I'd just started sorting the cutlery into the vintage coffee cans on my counter when Hector put down the phone, stalked over and slumped down on the nearest chair.

'So, it's just the two of us for Christmas dinner, then, Sophie.' He sounded glum.

'Why? I hope your parents are okay? They're not poorly, are they?'

Billy sat up straighter, his interest piqued.

'P'raps they've had a better offer. That brother of yours flying them down to his place?'

Hector sighed.

'No. But Mum just told me they've been persuaded at the last minute to volunteer on Christmas Day. They'll be serving meals to elderly neighbours who live on their own. She asked if we'd mind, and of course I couldn't object.'

'Then you must come to mine, Hector,' I said, hoping I didn't sound as pleased as I felt. I get on well with Hector's parents, but I'd been daunted at the prospect of spending Christmas Day with them. 'Christmas dinner in my cottage will be lovely and cosy.'

Hector pointed to the ceiling, indicating his flat above the shop.

'But my place is more private. As it's upstairs, we're not over-looked.'

I started folding paper napkins on the counter.

'But I like being able to see families going past the window on their Christmas Day walks, and the kids on new bikes and scooters.'

I hoped the thought of sharing our turkey with my little black cat, Blossom, wasn't putting him off. Hector is a dog person.

'There's always The Bluebird,' put in Billy. 'You're welcome to join me at my table.'

Without replying, Hector returned to the trade counter to serve a young woman with an armful of children's books.

Billy leaned towards me and tapped the side of his nose.

'Trust me, girlie,' he said in a low voice, 'if you want a restful Christmas, use your feminine wiles to get lover boy there to treat you to Christmas dinner at the pub. It'll save you time and trouble, and you won't have to worry about burning the turkey or singeing your sprouts.'

I wasn't sure which of Billy's assumptions offended me more: that I'd do all the cooking or that I lacked the necessary skills. Then I realised it had been a few weeks since we'd last eaten at the pub, and suddenly it seemed a long time since breakfast.

'Perhaps we'll look at Donald's Christmas menu tonight. Besides, aren't the St Bride's School carol singers due to come to Wendlebury then? That'll get us all feeling nice and festive.'

Billy sucked his teeth in apparent disapproval.

'Bloomin' posh kids. I don't know why they always come a-begging round here. Though to give 'em their due, they do sing like angels, unlike our church choir.' Frank, the choirmaster, insists on welcoming all who want to sing. His inclusive approach produces some interesting results. 'Of course, they don't have Walter One-note to contend with.'

To be fair, Walter is always word-perfect, but tends to anchor the choir like the great tenor bell in our parish church tower, striking a single low note while the smaller bells ring the changes.

I wondered what the boarding schoolgirls made of Billy. But before I had a chance to defend them or Walter, a couple of tourists waved to me from another table, and I grabbed my pad to take their order.

***

As we made our way from my cottage back up the High Street towards The Bluebird, I snuggled up to Hector for warmth. The weather had turned even colder since I'd come home from work, and Hector must have got chilled through walking down from the shop to call for me.

'It may be cold, but at least it's peaceful and pretty,' I remarked.

Hector stopped walking to gaze about us and raised a declamatory hand.

"'*'Tis calm indeed, so calm that it disturbs*
And vexes meditation with its strange
And extreme silentness.'"

'Eh?' I said.

"'*The secret ministry of frost*
Shall hang them up in silent icicles
Quietly shining to the quiet moon.'"

'Coleridge,' he added cheerfully, resuming his brisk walk. '*Frost at Midnight*. Lovely poem. One of my favourites.'

'Oh yes, of course. And speaking of frost, don't you love Robert Frost's poem about snow?'

Hector nodded.

'*Stopping by Woods on a Snowy Evening:*
"*But I have promises to keep,*
And miles to go before I sleep".'

'At least Coleridge didn't have to venture out into the cold night. He stayed indoors, writing by the hearth, and watching over his baby son asleep in his cot. We can go there, you know.'

It was my turn to stop abruptly in my tracks.

'What, you mean have a baby?' In the chilly air, my voice rang out louder than intended. I'd been wondering lately what a family Christmas would be like if Hector and I had children, but I hadn't dared mention it to him. I wasn't sure if either of us was ready for that. We hadn't even spent a Christmas Day together yet.

Hector coughed and ran his free hand over his mouth, as if to erase his last remark.

'No, to Coleridge's cottage, I mean. It's not far from my folks, off the Minehead road. It's owned by the National Trust now, and his sitting room looks as if he's just stepped out for a moment. Even his baby's cradle is still there, or at least an authentic replica.'

'But not his baby,' I added, trying to make light of my misunderstanding, while secretly picturing an old-fashioned cradle beside the hearth in my own sitting room, Hector working on one of his novels at my aunt's writing desk nearby.

I was grateful when Hector took the conversation off at a tangent, dispersing any awkwardness.

'Which would you rather go for a walk in, frost or snow?'

'Frost,' I said at once. 'It's much prettier. Beneath the full moon tonight, it's as if the village has been dusted in the finest glitter – the cars, the pavement, and the drystone walls. Those evergreens in Mrs Mill's front garden look as if they've been dipped in egg white and rolled in powdered sugar, like they do to cocktail glasses in fancy bars.'

Hector wrinkled his nose.

'Promise you'll never try that with my brandy. Anyway, don't let yourself be deceived by how pretty it looks. Frost is a mixed blessing in the Cotswolds. If the temperature dips below zero soon after rain, the drystone walls shatter as the water they've wicked up expands to form ice. By tomorrow morning, there'll be cascades of stone tumbling from the walls onto the pavements. Still, it keeps George Wall in business.'

I let go of his arm to pull my forget-me-not blue beret down over my ears, which were starting to turn numb.

'Surely Wall isn't his real name?'

'No, it's Walinski. He's from Poland, but he's made a nice niche for himself around here as a drystone waller. He's in work all year round.'

We turned up the pub's front path just in time to see the St Bride's School minibus reversing away from the car park entrance to avoid driving across sheet ice on the tarmac. From within the minibus came a muffled roar of enthusiasm from the excited girls, who were waving and hammering on the windows to attract our attention. We waved back as PE teacher Joe Spryke completed a neat three-point turn before rejoining the main road to park beside the village green.

'It's too cold to stay out here to listen to them,' said Hector. 'We'll catch them when they do their set inside the pub.'

When he held open the door of The Bluebird for me to go in first, a golden glow spilled out into the frosty night, reminding me of old paintings of a light-filled stable beneath Bethlehem's dark skies. I glanced up, almost expecting to see a single bright star above the pub roof, before remonstrating with myself for blasphemy – me, a Sunday school teacher too, and author of the previous year's village Nativity play. The play hadn't gone according to plan, but at least it all ended happily.

The good-natured noise within the pub soon distracted me from any thoughts of that dramatic debacle. Almost all the tables were taken by lively groups of family and friends, including several staff outings from Bristol firms, seeking the cosy delights of a traditional country pub in winter.

In the darts corner, Billy had just thrown the deciding shot in a match. He staggered slightly as he passed his empty tankard to his opponent, claiming the refill that was his prize. As he spotted our arrival, he steadied himself on the back of the nearest chair.

'Evening, Sophie, evening, Hector!' He gave us a cheery wave. 'If you want a masterclass in how to spend a convivial evening without ever having to put your hand in your pocket, come and join me.'

Hector tutted as we headed for the last empty table on the opposite side of the room.

'Tomorrow, sweetheart, you'd better make Billy's elevenses a black coffee.'

***

Just as we had finished our plates of delicious chicken casserole, the front door opened wide to admit a crowd of pink-cheeked St Bride's girls, led by Louisa Price, their music teacher. Then came Gemma Lamb, the English teacher, and her boyfriend Joe Spryke. We knew most of the school staff and some of the girls from their visits to the bookshop and tearoom. After their traditional carolling tour of the village, the girls had come to warm up singing in the pub. Donald set down on the bar the tray of refreshments he'd had ready for them: large glasses of wine for Louisa and Gemma, small ones for the older girls, and soft drinks for the younger pupils and Joe as designated driver. No-one was more pleased to see the carol singers than Donald.

'Come on, girls, let's start with my favourite!'

He folded his arms and leaned on the bar to enjoy their performance. Even the hubbub in the darts corner quietened down to allow the lilting melody of 'Three Kings from Persian Lands Afar' to soar up to the old oak rafters.

When that carol was over, Donald brought us our puddings, and we addressed ourselves to fragrant ginger sponge and velvety custard to the tune of 'Past Three O'Clock'.

During the third carol, 'As with Gladness Men of Old', a couple of the girls began to circulate among the tables, rattling red collecting boxes for the charity Shelter. Most people willingly contributed, but as Polly held her box out to Billy, he thrust both hands behind his back.

'You can't expect a poor old man like me to subsidise the likes of you,' he protested. 'Christmas is a costly time. I'm saving my cash to pay for my Christmas dinner.'

'Go on, you mean old goat,' said Bert, one of his darts chums. 'You've not had to buy a drink all night. You're positively rattling with spare change. Anyway, they're not collecting for themselves, like we used to do when we were nippers. Look at their collection box: it's for the homeless. Whatever else you are, you're not homeless. Cough up and be done with it.'

Hands on his hips, Billy turned on Bert.

'It's not as if these girlies can't put in money of their own. They're all loaded. Remember, I used to be a gardener up at St Bride's, and I've seen their parents dropping them off in fancy cars. If these kiddies want to raise money for a charity, they should get their dads to flog their personalised numberplates and chuck the proceeds in the pot. I'd let 'em keep the cars.'

His tone of voice suggested he thought that a generous concession.

The pub had fallen silent for the first time since we'd arrived. Bert clapped Billy on the back.

'Come on, Bill, no need to be like that. Sorry, girls. Don't mind him, silly old git.'

Louisa stepped forward to address Billy, her clear, authoritative teacher's voice ringing out for all to hear.

'The parents' cars are irrelevant. The girls are contributing to the cause themselves. It's a St Bride's tradition that any pocket money left over by the end of this term goes into their chosen Christmas charity.

You can be sure every girl in the school has donated from her own purse.'

As Gemma was standing close to our table, I took the opportunity to put in a quiet word on Billy's behalf. 'Please excuse him, Gemma. That's just the drink talking. Billy's actually very kind. He's been nothing but generous to me since I came to live in Wendlebury, and he's always helping village kids.'

Fortunately, Gemma had seen Billy in the tearoom when he was sober and relatively well behaved.

'Don't worry, Sophie, I'm sure the girls will take it in their stride. Besides, it looks like his mates are putting in extra money to make up for his refusal, so I reckon we'll come out ahead.'

Donald was less forgiving. He lifted the bar counter flap and strode across the room to lay a hand firmly on Billy's shoulder.

'I think you've had enough for one evening, Bill. I suggest you go home and have a spot of supper to mop up all that free beer you've been quaffing.'

He marched Billy to the back door to avoid being seen decanting a drunk onto the High Street. Billy remained unrepentant.

''Tis better to give than to receive,' he called to the girls over his shoulder. 'Easier for a rich man than a camel. Or the eye of the thread.'

The girls giggled at his slurred mangling of the familiar Bible quote, suggesting his rant hadn't upset them. Then they returned their empty glasses to the bar and trooped out after Louisa to sing a few more carols on the village green before returning to their school.

***

When Donald eventually came to remove our empty pudding bowls, he was still trying to justify having chucked Billy out for being drunk, even though he was only following licensing laws.

'Billy never stays much later than this anyway. He's always been early to bed, early to rise. Raised by his mother who was raised by candlelight, he told me once, and she always kept the same hours as the sun. Just as well my customers aren't all like that or I'd be broke.'

Hector had been reading an interesting book about the history of sleep, and for days he'd been quoting odd facts.

'Why do you think we call twelve o'clock midnight?' he said now to Donald. 'In the olden days, we would have been halfway through our night's sleep.'

Donald looked wistful. 'I should be so lucky.'

'Poor Donald,' I said, watching him return to the bar. 'I bet he never gets enough sleep in a job like his.'

Hector touched his foot against mine under the table. 'Now that gives me an idea. Fancy an early night, sweetheart?'

Before I could reply, an anguished shout came from the back door. Bert had just flung the door open after going out to smoke a roll-up in the car park.

'Quick! Someone help! Billy's spreadeagled on the ice, and I can't get any sense out of him.'

Hector and I were first to reach Billy. Then Joe Spryke and three of the St Bride's girls came running along the lane from the village green where they'd gone to sing their last few carols. They must have heard Bert's anguished cry when he discovered Billy's prostrate body in the car park.

Kneeling on the tarmac, I realised the hard ground was cold enough to penetrate through Billy's thin overcoat. His eyes were closed, his body motionless.

'Billy!' I grabbed one of his ungloved hands and wrapped both mine around it for warmth. 'Stay with us, Billy!'

His head lolled towards me, then his eyes half-opened, making me gasp in surprise. He squinted at me for a moment.

'You're no angel!' he declared, sounding as if he felt short-changed.

Hector, kneeling beside me, snorted with laughter, probably from relief at seeing a sign of life.

'I never said I was,' I replied, hoping Billy hadn't noticed my silent tears.

When Hector put his arm around Billy's shoulders ready to raise him into a sitting position, one of the girls, Polly, put her hand on his shoulder to stop him.

'Don't move him yet, Mr Munro. Not till we've checked his vital signs and looked for broken bones.' She turned to one of her friends. 'Katie, can you please go back into the pub and ask Donald to lend us some blankets?'

Katie paused only to slip off her own coat and spread it over Billy's body before making a dash for the back door.

Billy eyed Polly with suspicion as she lifted his wrist to take his pulse. 'You're no nurse, neither. You're just a kiddie.'

'Not as such, but we've just done first aid as an extra this term, and you're the perfect guinea pig for us to practise on.'

I'm constantly astonished at what useful skills the girls learn at St Bride's

Polly turned to the other girl. 'Suki, where's your torch?'

As the girls launched a flurry of tests, Joe crouched down and cupped his hands round Billy's reddened face to warm it. Billy began to ramble.

'Do you know, as I lay here just now, I heard angels singing, angels bending near the earth. I knew it couldn't be the church choir because there weren't no Walter One-note. Unfurling their wings, they were, and such wings, soft and white as a washing powder advert, sparkling in the moonlight!'

As Katie returned with an armful of blankets, Hector and I exchanged concerned glances.

'The stars in the sky were twinkling, like the angels had left a trail of silver dust where they'd descended from the heavens. They were coming to sing me to sleep, while the good Lord looked down from above with his great moon face.'

Polly slipped a slender hand beneath his shirt and pullover to feel his chest.

'Hmm, his body temperature's a bit low, so I'm not surprised he's confused. But at least his heartbeat is sound, and his breathing isn't at all laboured.'

Suki switched off her torch. 'Dilated pupils too, so good news all round. If he had extreme hypothermia, his pupils wouldn't be reactive to light. I think it's safe to say it's a mild case. After all, he hasn't been out here very long. If we warm him up gradually and thoroughly, he should be all right.'

'Well done, girls,' said a familiar voice, and I looked up to see that Gemma had come to stand beside me, leaving Louisa conducting the final carol of the evening. 'Billy must have heard you girls singing on the village green,' she said. 'Mistaking your voices for a heavenly choir is as high an accolade as you can get. Miss Price will be chuffed about that. But, Joe, we really need to get the girls back to school. They've got to pack tonight before they go home for the holidays in the morning. Sophie, can you and Hector see Billy home safely?'

'Sure,' I said. 'His cottage is only just down the lane.'

Joe patted me on the shoulder in appreciation.

'Good thing the girls covered hypothermia in their extra lesson last week. I thought December was a good time to teach it to them, but I didn't expect they'd need to deploy their new skills and knowledge so soon.'

'Lucky it wasn't our term for car maintenance, Billy, or else we'd have had to jump-start you,' said Suki.

Her friends giggled.

'Or change your spark plugs,' added Katie, laughing.

'You leave my spark plugs alone,' grumbled Billy, a welcome indication that he was starting to perk up.

With Hector and me supporting him on either side, he rose unsteadily to his feet.

'I don't have the words to thank you girlies,' he was saying. 'If only I had some mince pies or even biscuits at my cottage, I'd invite you back for a proper thank you.'

Gemma waved her hand dismissively.

'That's very kind, but the girls are just glad to have been of help. Aren't you, girls?'

'Yes, miss,' they chorused.

Billy dipped his hands deep into his trouser pockets, brought out two handfuls of small change, which he held out to the girls.

'Here, put that little lot in your collection box. I don't know what I was thinking when I said all that nonsense earlier. I pity anyone who must sleep outside on a night like this. Though strange to say, if it hadn't been for them angels singing, if I'd lain here much longer, I think I'd have drifted off to sleep myself.'

'Falling asleep without a care: classic symptom and outcome of hypothermia,' said Suki, now serious. 'And it's a sleep they don't wake up from.'

Just then, Donald came marching across to join us, clutching his mobile phone. I didn't know what had kept him so long – perhaps fear of what he might find.

I'd misjudged him. He'd been on the phone to the local doctor.

'I've tracked down Dr Hastings,' he informed us. 'He's at his son's house in Slate Green just now, but he'd be happy to call in on Billy when he gets back to give him the once over if you like. But he said we shouldn't hesitate to call an ambulance if we think it's necessary.'

'I'm not going nowhere in no ambulance!' cried Billy. 'If they takes me off in one of them things, I may never see my cottage again!'

Suki shook her head.

'If the patient refuses to go, an ambulance won't take him. If the emergency services hear someone saying they don't want an ambulance, they won't even send one out for you.' She raised a forefinger. 'But here's a handy tip: if you're ever in that position, just say the patient has had a blow to the head and isn't in a fit state to make decisions. Then they'll have to come.'

Donald raised his eyebrows at Billy.

'I'm storing that up for future reference, Bill. A blow to the head can be arranged if you start any more of your malarkey.'

As Hector and I began to escort Billy home, the girls headed back to the village green, their crisp accents carrying perfectly in the still night air.

'Shame there wasn't any paradoxical undressing,' Suki was saying as they left the car park.

'Para what?' asked one of her friends.

'You know, in severe hypothermia when people start taking off their clothes.'

I was thankful Billy hadn't got that far.

***

Once we were inside Billy's cottage, I headed for the kitchen to boil the kettle and make a pot of tea, while in the sitting room, Hector stripped off Billy's damp outer layers. For the sake of the old man's dignity, Hector covered him with blankets from a pile on the end of the sofa, before bringing me Billy's wet clothes to hang up to dry on the ceiling rack.

Then I filled a hot water bottle that I'd spotted hanging from a nail on the back of the kitchen door and took it into Billy to apply to whatever part of his body needed it most. Hector followed behind with the tea tray, which he set within Billy's reach on the hearth, before stoking up the embers of the log fire and adding a few sticks and a big log.

'While you drink your tea, can I fetch your pyjamas and dressing gown from your bedroom?' I suggested.

Billy stared into the fire as it started to catch.

'I ain't got one.'

'What, no bedroom?' I didn't mean to sound so shocked.

'No, pyjamas and stuff. Of course, I've got a bedroom, but at this time of year, I prefers to kip on the sofa at night in me clothes.' That explained the pile of blankets. 'I mean, what's the point in wasting the embers of the fire downstairs by sleeping in a cold bedroom?'

'No central heating,' Hector mouthed to me behind Billy's back.

I had no answer to that, so sought another way to warm him up.

'Then what can I cook for you to eat? Have you any tins of soup?'

Billy groaned.

'I ain't got much in food wise just now. Don't worry about me. Just give me an extra big slice of cake with my elevenses tomorrow.'

I frowned. 'That won't do, Billy. You need a hot meal inside you tonight. Hector, can you run back up to the pub and see whether Donald's got any of that chicken casserole left?'

Billy licked his lips, giving away just how hungry he really was.

While Hector was gone, I kept Billy talking to make sure he was properly himself after his earlier confusion. His monologue about the right way to build the perfect fire (as opposed to Hector's technique) assured me he was back to normal.

As soon as Hector returned, Billy tucked hungrily into Donald's casserole.

'Maybe that's why I slipped earlier,' he said, scraping the last drop up with his soupspoon. 'Insufficient ballast. Hadn't had no tea before I went to the pub.'

'Speaking of eating,' said Hector, 'I'm afraid there's bad news about your proposed Christmas dinner at The Bluebird. Donald just told me he and his wife are taking Christmas Day off. They're exhausted, poor souls. They'll be closing at midnight on Christmas Eve and not reopening until Boxing Day.'

'The lazy lumps!' cried Billy. 'Now what am I to do?'

I knew Carol's shelves were overflowing with festive goods.

'I'm sure you'll find everything you need for a Christmas dinner in the village shop.'

'Not a working oven, I won't,' said Billy. 'How am I meant to roast a turkey when the only things in my kitchen that aren't bust are the kettle and the toaster?'

I caught Hector's eye, and he gave me a scarcely perceptible nod. 'In that case, you're very welcome to join me and Hector for Christmas dinner. A turkey's far too big for two people, anyway, even allowing plenty for Blossom.'

Billy looked from me to Hector. 'You sure, boy? I don't want to be in the way of you and love's young dream here.'

'Don't worry about us,' said Hector, reaching for my hand. 'We'll have plenty more Christmases together, won't we, Sophie?'

I smiled and squeezed his hand.

'Yes, I think we will.'

***

The day after his icy fall, when he opened his front door to take in his morning pint of milk, Billy found a large cardboard box on his doorstep. Inside lay a sturdy Christmas cake, topped with three white fondant angels playing golden harps. The enclosed card from Suki explained that all the girls at St Bride's had made Christmas cakes, and as her younger sister was also a pupil, and their family didn't need two cakes, he'd be doing them a favour by taking the spare one off her hands. Also in the box was a bag of mince pies of different shapes and sizes from all the girls in the choir. They'd donated one each from the batches they'd made to take home to their families.

Then on Christmas Day, under my Christmas tree – the tree that I'd bought from Billy and Tommy Crowe, the lovable teenage rogue who was his sidekick of the moment, just a couple of weeks before – lay two squishy parcels with Billy's name on: jaunty Royal Stewart tartan brushed-cotton pyjamas from me and a midnight-blue fleecy dressing gown from Hector.

These weren't the only treats that lay in store for Billy that day. Following an elaborate roast turkey dinner at my cottage, with turkey sandwiches and Dundee cake at Hector's flat later in the day, waiting for him by his front gate when he got home that evening was a large brown-paper parcel with The Bluebird's compliments slip sellotaped to it. Inside was an expensive pair of Wellington boots with extra deep tread to guard against any more slips.

'There's someone with a guilty conscience,' said Billy wryly, when he told us about his new boots next time we saw him. 'I bet in future Donald will be scattering a lot more salt in his car park during cold snaps.' He gazed at his wellies for a moment before looking up me. 'You know, I wasn't wrong about the angels watching over me that night. But now I've learned that in real life, angels ain't necessarily got wings.'

This story was inspired by the lyrics of the Christmas carol 'It Came Upon a Midnight Clear' by Edmund Sears.

Travels with My Aunt's Garden: The Poinsettia

Sophie Sayers' column for the December issue of the Wendlebury Barrow Parish News.

When I was a little girl, and my Great Auntie May was still travelling the world on her quest for articles for magazines and Sunday supplements, and journalling notes to be turned into books, she would send me an unusual Christmas present from wherever she happened to be towards the end of each calendar year. Her gift was always a novelty that could not be found in a British toyshop, and I'd never be able to guess from the packaging what it might be.

My favourite was a small fabric doll with skin the colour of butterscotch and thick black woollen hair, plaited into two long braids. The end of each braid was tied with red ribbon, then tied again to its beginning, each hoop of hair secured with a white cotton bow behind her ear. I thought this an incredibly glamorous hairstyle and immediately vowed to grow my shoulder-length hair long enough to mimic it. Her simple white cotton tunic was embroidered with scarlet cross stitches at the cuffs, neckline and hem, and a pillar-box red shawl was attached to her shoulders with tiny hidden stitches.

'Is she meant to be Little Red Riding Hood?' I asked my mum, stroking those long plaits. 'If so, her shawl ought to have a hood.'

Mum tried to read the label, but it was in Spanish.

'I don't know, but those red flowers she's holding are poinsettias. I've never seen those in any of your fairy-tale books.'

She touched the pointy red petals arrayed, star-like, around a cluster of custard-yellow cotton French knots.

'Not flowers, love,' said Dad. 'Technically speaking, the red bits are leaves. The yellow dots are the flowers.'

'Are you sure?' said Mum, and Dad nodded.

I found that as hard to believe as when he told me the yolk of the egg wasn't the part that became the chick, but the food supply for the embryo. I'd assumed it was a daft dad joke that the opaque squiggle suspended between the yolk and the white would eventually turn into the baby bird. Only in biology class at secondary school did I finally believe him.

'Why has she got green leaves in her other hand, then?' I asked him. 'Or are you going to tell me those are flowers too?'

Dad shrugged, his knowledge of festive flowers exhausted. He bought Mum roses every Christmas.

'I don't know. They look like weeds to me.'

'Well, I'm going to call them leaves and the red ones flowers,' I decided.

'I suppose the red leaves do look like a child's drawing of a flower,' he conceded.

I wasn't sure whether to be pleased or offended by that.

For want of a better name, I decided to call my new doll Poinsettia. After all, I had a white teddy bear called Daisy, and a pink cat called Rose, so another floral name would match theirs.

***

It wasn't until Great Auntie May came to visit us the following summer that I discovered the truth about my doll. I'd brought her down from my bedroom to welcome her, thinking Poinsettia might like to be reunited with her giver.

'Auntie May, why is Poinsettia holding leaves in one hand and flowers in the other?' I asked.

'Did you not see the explanatory note I put in the family Christmas card?' She glanced reprovingly at Mum. 'Then I'd better tell you again.'

Drawing me and my doll onto her lap, she told me this story:

There was once a little girl in Mexico who was so poor she couldn't afford to buy a present to take to her village church in the Christmas Eve procession. Everyone else had gifts to offer the Baby Jesus, but she had nothing. Then an angel appeared to her and told her that it didn't matter what she gave him, so long as she gave it with love in her heart. So she brought what she could find for free: armfuls of the green weeds that grew in abundance at the roadside, and she laid them before the crib.

As soon as she had set them down, the green weeds turned a brilliant red. At the centre of each group of red leaves lay a tiny cluster of yellow flowers, reminding all who saw them of the star that shone down that first Christmas night to guide the poor shepherds to the stable to worship their new-born king.

'What mattered was not how much her gift had cost, but how much love was in her heart,' explained Auntie May. 'Mexican legend says it was a Christmas miracle.'

'Would Scottish weeds do that if Dad gave them to Mum with enough love in his heart?' I asked.

Dad scoffed. 'I think I'd get short shrift from your mother if I brought her a bunch of weeds and thistles.'

Auntie May raised her eyebrows at him. 'Don't you remember bringing me dandelions when you were a little boy?'

For a moment he looked blank, and then the recollection returned. 'So I did, until the boy next door told me picking dandelions made you wet the bed.'

The corners of her mouth turned up, her smile mischievous. '*Le pissenlit*, the French call the dandelion. The wee-in-the-bed.'

I shrieked with laughter. 'And did it make you wee in the bed, Dad?'

'I don't recall,' Dad mumbled.

I returned my attention to Auntie May. 'These yellow flowers aren't dandelions, though, are they? Dandelions are yellow all over. These are a lovely Christmassy red.'

With the tip of her little fingernail, Auntie May touched the tiny French knots in yellow embroidery thread at the centre of each fabric poinsettia. 'In Mexico, they're called the Flor de Nochebuena, which means the Christmas Eve Flower. I've also heard them called the Flower of the Holy Night, or the Flame Flower or the Christmas Star. Whatever name you prefer, they grow wild all over Mexico and Central America, and they were once cultivated by an ancient civilisation called the Aztecs for medicinal purposes and for their beauty.

'Then one day in the nineteenth century, an American politician came down from the USA, one Mr Poinsett. He was the US Ambassador to Mexico. He took a fancy to this colourful, cheery plant, and who can blame him? After he sent samples back home, it went on to be widely cultivated and marketed as a festive plant for its bright colour in the depths of winter. For the US market, it was named in his honour, becoming the poinsettia, masking the Mexican legend of its origins.'

I looked at my Mexican doll in horror.

'I don't want to call her after a conceited man like that,' I declared. 'What else could I call her? What are little girls called who live in Mexico?'

My aunt considered for a moment. She'd spent a lot of time in Mexico and must have known plenty of real people there.

'Juanita? Lavinia? Maria? Lucida? Rosa?'

I made my doll nod her head.

'That'll do. I'll call her all of those from now on. Could you please write them down, so I don't forget?'

She obliged.

Ever since, when I see poinsettias appearing in shops at Christmas time, I must suppress the urge to cross the name off the signs and graffiti my doll's name over the top.

It was to my aunt's regret that she couldn't plant the Flor de Nochebuena in her cottage garden in Wendlebury Barrow. It would quickly perish, she told me, in our erratic Cotswold climate, needing a constant eighteen degrees Celsius, so instead she nurtured a potted one indoors, from year to year. I don't have her green fingers, but each year I buy a new one, and each year, Juanita Lavinia Maria Lucida Rosa sits beside it on the windowsill, in honour of my Great Auntie May.

One last thought: for the poinsettia's green leaves to turn red in time for Christmas, it needs at least 12 hours of darkness each night, In Mexico at Christmas time, the sun rises at 7am and sets at 6pm.

Festive miracle or plain old biological science? I know which I prefer to believe.

Christmas Ginger

'Christmas tree, May Sayers?' Billy wrapped his arms across his chest for warmth as he stood on my doorstep. 'I've just got one littl'un left that's a steal at twenty quid.'

At the far end of my front path, his handcart of festive evergreens was blocking the pavement, its load much depleted since his visit the previous week. His assistant, a scruffy teenage boy, was nowhere to be seen, but that was not surprising as it was Christmas Eve.

Billy began to stamp his feet to boost his circulation. 'I can bring it in and help you set it up, if you like, May.'

It had been decades since I decorated a Christmas tree. In my younger days, I left it to my parents. Since retiring from my peripatetic career as a travel writer, I've spent my Christmases with my nephew and his family in Inverness. By the time I arrive there, his wife and daughter Sophie have already set their tree up. But this year, for the first time ever, a snowstorm in Scotland had scuppered my plans and I'd be spending Christmas alone in my cottage.

'Well, why not, Billy? It would give me something to do. I think my mother's old box of baubles is still in the cupboard under the stairs. While you bring it in, I'll put the kettle on. You look like you could do with a cup of tea to warm you up.'

'Shall I add some mistletoe to your order?' Billy gave me a cheeky wink. 'You never know when you might get lucky.'

I fixed him with an old-fashioned look. 'I'll give the mistletoe a miss, thank you, Billy.'

Like me, Billy had never married. As he'd lived all his life in the village, the local girls of our vintage saw him more as a brotherly type than as husband material, and a naughty little brother at that. What miles I had put between us, pursuing my career far away from Wendlebury Barrow since we were at school together.

Once Billy had heaved the tree into my parlour, he set it up in front of the window. My wastepaper basket provided a makeshift pot, and he wedged it into position with a few bits of kindling from the hearth. I rewarded him with a cup of tea and a slice of the Christmas cake I'd bought from Carol at the village shop the previous afternoon, when I'd realised I'd be spending the festive period at home.

'I thought you finished selling your Christmas trees a week ago, Billy.'

He replied through a mouthful of crumbs. 'Aye, but I didn't have enough mistletoe to go round last week, so I'm dropping off some orders before I packs up for the season. I had this one little tree left over needing a good home. Then when I stopped in the village shop just now for a box of matches, Carol Barker told me your trip up north was off, so I thought I'd bring it down to you. You must be put out, now you won't be seeing that little cutie of yours.'

As I stirred my tea, watching the whirlpool I'd created, I pictured the River Ness, feeling the pull of its waters as they rushed out to the Moray Firth on their way to the North Sea. When Sophie was little, I'd hold her hand on our riverside walks, nervous of her stumbling into currents that could so easily bear her away from me. I confess I was afraid of a British river – I, who had stood beneath the spray of the

Niagara Falls, crossed the Zambezi on a rickety rope bridge, paddled down the Amazon in a canoe, all without a thought for my own safety. On my last few trips to Scotland, Sophie had felt too old to hold my hand, looping her arm companionably through mine instead.

'What's her name again? Suki, isn't it? Or Susie?' Billy was saying. Sophie had been spending her summer holidays with me since she became old enough to stay away from her parents for any length of time, so he'd seen her about the village. 'What's up, you two fallen out?'

'You mean Sophie. And no, it's the weather that's keeping us apart, Billy. Inverness Airport is snowed in and unlikely to reopen for days.'

'Why don't you just drive up there? Save all that hanging around at airports.'

I sighed. He meant well.

'I'm afraid I don't have the stamina for such a long drive these days. It's the best part of a day's journey by car even in midsummer. Besides, if the airport's closed, it's likely the A9 will be impassable.'

Billy looked blank.

'Why, do they park the planes on it when they're not using them?'

As Billy seldom leaves the parish and doesn't drive, he has only the haziest idea about long-distance road travel. Even locally, he refers to roads by their traditional names rather than the official road numbers: the Fosse Way, the Bath Road, the old London Road.

'The A9 would be the final part of my journey by car, heading north from Central Scotland. It runs all the way from Falkirk to Scrabster Harbour on the north coast. It's a high road, very exposed, so prone to snowdrifts. At the roadside, there are poles to indicate the depth of the snow. Once it reaches a certain height, they close the snow gates until it's safe to drive again.'

When Billy held out his empty cup in the direction of the teapot, I took the hint and refilled it.

'It's not like you to be so defeatist, May Sayers. What's wrong with the train? You're not short of a bob or two. Why don't you spend some of your money on a train ticket? You can get a train almost all the way from Land's End to John O'Groats. I've seen it on the telly.'

My lips twitched into my first smile of the day.

'And get stuck in a train in a snowdrift? Have you never read *Murder on the Orient Express*?'

Billy chortled. 'No, but I seen the film. So Hercule Poirot's not your type?' He leaned forward to prod my knee with a grubby forefinger. 'But we all know who is, don't we?'

My cheeks began to burn, and not from the fire.

'Oh, for goodness' sake, Billy, that was decades ago, when he and I were both young, free and single.'

He drained his cup and set it in its saucer on the coffee table with a clatter.

'Well, now you're both old, free, and single. You sure I can't interest you in a bit of mistletoe just in case? I ain't got much left to get rid of before I can get home to my fireside.'

I fished my purse out of my handbag and found a twenty-pound note to pay him for the tree.

'Well, if you hadn't stopped for tea, cake and gossip with every delivery, you'd have got home a lot quicker.'

As he pocketed my payment, he frowned. 'What sort of a scrounger do you take me for? I haven't had tea and cake at every stop. I had a smoked salmon sandwich at the vicarage, and very nice it was too.'

He patted his round tummy before buttoning his ancient tweed jacket across it and rising to his feet.

'Why aren't you wearing an overcoat, Billy? Or at least a scarf, hat, and gloves. You want to wrap up warmer at your age.'

He guffawed. 'You mean our age.'

I followed him to the hall. As he opened the front door, a gust of icy wind made us catch our breath.

Billy braced himself to step out into the cold. 'We'll be having snow ourselves before too long, you mark my words.'

I took down from the hallstand a colourful stripey scarf, woven by an old Turkish lady in a tiny, rough cottage where I'd once spent the night. I wasn't keen on the colours, but I'd bought it to supplement the paltry fee she was charging for my accommodation. The scarf had hung on the hallstand ever since I'd brought it home, reminding me every day of the contrast between her home and mine.

As Billy turned to say goodbye, I looped the Turkish scarf about his neck.

'Merry Christmas, Billy.'

I stepped quickly back inside before he could get the wrong idea. He'd never caught me at kiss-chase in the playground, and I wasn't about to let him start now.

His face lit up in delighted surprise.

'Why, thank you very much, May Sayers, that's most kind.'

Tucking its ends inside his jacket, he bustled down my front path to retrieve his cart. As he headed off to finish his mistletoe rounds, he was still smiling.

And so was I.

***

As soon as I'd closed the front door, I dragged my mother's old box of Christmas decorations out from the cupboard under the stairs. I'd have decorated my little tree faster if I hadn't stopped to reminisce about the origin of each bauble as I took it from the box.

These days, people think nothing of buying new decorations each year. I swear Sophie's mother throws hers out come January, because I've never seen their Christmas trees look the same twice. My parents kept every single bauble from year to year, protecting the wafer-thin glass with layer upon layer of newspaper. Unwrapping them now was like playing the children's party game of Pass the Parcel. Just like Mother used to do, I flattened each piece of newspaper as I took it off. At the end of the process, just as she did, I laid the pile of sheets back in the box, ready to receive the baubles again on Twelfth Night.

Some of the newspapers dated back to the Second World War and were frailer than the decorations. A few of them were in foreign languages. I recognised the Egyptian newspaper in which I'd wrapped a ceramic ashtray I'd brought my parents from Cairo.

When I came home that Christmas, Mother and Father had been expecting me to settle down and marry Joshua, the boy next door – now the elderly gentleman next door. As I smoothed out the last piece of newspaper, I noticed the skin on the back of my hands was papery too. Back then, Joshua had beautiful hands, supple and bronzed from his active outdoor life. These days, they'd probably be as delicate as mine. But they'd still be Joshua's hands.

I'd had to break it to all three of them that my return was only temporary. Straight after New Year, I was due to take up a part-time office job at the British Embassy in Cairo. The post came with a nice bedsitting room in a safe compound, where I could spend my free time writing. But the biggest perk of my new job had come the following March, when, serving drinks to guests at an Embassy reception, I got chatting to the visiting features editor of a British newspaper. Taking a shine to me, he commissioned my first column, which turned into a monthly spot. After a year, my track record with the newspaper made it relatively easy for me to secure a publishing contract for my first book. Its title was simply *Cairo*. It did very well and was to become the first in a series about ancient capital cities.

Meanwhile, Joshua continued to write me long and frequent letters, full of love and hope and expectation. To my shame, I replied sporadically and only by postcard, too caught up in my new career to think far beyond the vibrant, bustling city that was flooding my senses.

While I went on to travel the world, ever thirsty for new places and fresh faces, Joshua stayed in Wendlebury in the house where he'd been born. Before long, Edith, the pretty new barmaid at The Blackbird, caught his eye – and the rest of him followed. When Mother wrote to tell me ruefully they planned to marry, I dismissed the news. A whirlwind romance on the rebound wouldn't last five minutes. I hadn't been gone that long. How could he have found a replacement for me so quickly?

Eventually, I realised time passes more slowly in Wendlebury Barrow. But by then, I had lost him forever.

After I'd hung the last bauble on the tree, I placed the Egyptian newspaper on top of the pile in the box. The Arabic characters conjured up the scents and sounds of Cairo, the adrenalin that fuelled my solo outings, and the strange new tastes and textures I encountered in the local cafés and bars. I've long since forgotten any Arabic I once knew, but the shapes of the words were familiar old friends. I had plenty of memories from my travels to treasure besides those of my lost love.

If I couldn't be in Scotland for Christmas, I could journey there in my head as easily as I could to Cairo, to Athens, to Patagonia, and everywhere else I'd ever travelled for my career. All over the house, souvenirs prompted memories of my many destinations. A watercolour of feluccas on the Nile hung just inside my front door; blue and white Chinese plates were displayed above the stairs; and the handwoven Persian rug I'd bought from its maker nestled beneath my feet in the front parlour. In my kitchen, I could sip mint tea from jewel-bright Moroccan tea-glasses and imagine myself back in the souks of Marrakech. Snacking on tapas from my Spanish pottery platter, bright with primary colours, I'd hear classical guitar tunes playing in my head.

One day soon, I must catalogue all these things, so that when I'm no longer here to explain their origin and value, they'll still be understood and treasured. Sophie is to have my cottage when I'm gone. Not that I'm letting on, as I want her to go out and make her own way in the world first, but when it's hers, I'd like her to know what's what.

The same goes for my garden. Not that I brought many plants back from abroad – import and export laws are too restrictive. Most of my plants have come from the nearest garden centre at Slate Green. But after I inherited my cottage from my parents, I planted something to reflect every trip I'd made, from a Japanese flowering cherry to an Australian eucalyptus. It was how I made the garden my own.

Now, before I did anything else, I needed to clear away the tea things from Billy's visit. As I set the tray on the draining board in the kitchen, I lingered by the window for a moment, admiring my imaginative planting scheme. In my parents' day, the garden had been an uncluttered rectangle divided into strips for growing vegetables, framed like a sampler by the original dry-stone walls. Now very little of the walls could be seen behind my flourishing trees, shrubs, and perennials. I hoped they were holding up against the weather. Cotswold stone wicks up rainwater like a sponge, and in a cold snap, ice forms inside it. As the ice expands, it shatters the stone from within.

As far as I could see now, the walls were still intact, even the weaker patch where there had once stood a gate between our garden and Joshua's. When Edith married him, she made him block it up, because that was where he and I used to meet in our teens. We'd spend the lazy hours of our summers lying on our backs in his garden or mine, in the shadow of our raspberry canes or his apple trees, cloud-gazing by day, watching for shooting stars at night. At least, that's what we told our parents.

The first time I came home after their wedding, the fresh blond stone plugging the gap had seemed unnecessary and a little spiteful. When I complained to my father, he gave a wry smile, quoting Robert Frost: *'Good fences make good neighbours.'*

Little did I know then that for years to come, Joshua would blow a kiss to every passing plane, just in case it was the one bearing me home. It didn't matter that I was always more likely to travel by train and ferry; it was his way of reaching out for me.

Those blond stones soon weathered to match the older part of the wall, thanks to Wendlebury's exposed position high on the rolling Cotswold hills. 'When it's jacket weather down in Slate Green, it's overcoat weather up in Wendlebury Barrow,' my father used to say. But I can still tell where the gate once was, even if no-one else can.

Not that it matters to Edith anymore, as she'd died the previous summer from a sudden heart attack. According to Carol, she fell to the floor like a domino as she was clearing away her tea things. She was gone before the ambulance arrived.

Now Joshua would be spending his first Christmas alone. Well, not entirely alone. He and Edith had not been blessed with children, and after their parents had died, his kind nephew always invited the two of them for Christmas. Then, after Edith's death, Joshua had gone alone.Padd At least Joshua could still get to his nephew's. There were no snowdrifts between Wendlebury and Bristol.

Closing the wooden shutters, I returned to the parlour to give myself a firm talking-to. I had plenty of food and drink in the house, and the radio, television, and books to keep me amused. There was a great stack of logs and a wicker basket overflowing with kindling on the hearth. The fire in the wood-burner was glowing cheerfully, reflected many times over in the pretty baubles on my tree.

Of course, there were no presents under the tree. Mine would be under Sophie's tree right now, awaiting my arrival. I'd packed my gifts to her family in my suitcase three days ago, and there they would stay, waiting for when my flight could be rebooked.

Fortunately, my nomadic career has equipped me with a useful knack for turning disrupted plans into opportunities. Some of my best reports sprang from serendipitous events rather than from carefully choreographed journeys. My story on the great Kefalonian earthquake of 1953 came about only because my ferry to Patras had been cancelled, leaving me wandering the streets in the wake of this terrible natural disaster. As I stayed longer, exploring the island and beyond, I wrote about a community abandoning its village, which had been damaged beyond repair. The article was syndicated around the world.

Half a century later, it had another lease of life in a follow-up piece. When I returned to light a candle in what I presumed to be the abandoned tiny Greek Orthodox Church in the ruined village, I found a lantern still burning. Someone returns each day to keep the flame alight, and I tracked them down. Their simple faith boosted mine.

Now I switched on the radio to listen to the traditional Carols from King's College, Cambridge. Singing along, I decided to do something constructive to lift my spirits. Whenever my travel plans were disrupted, I used to find it helpful to restore order to my immediate surroundings, perhaps by repacking my bag with immaculate precision, or by dusting my hotel room. As a traveller rather than a holidaymaker, I've stayed in plenty of places that had never seen a duster until I got there. I never packed a duster in my luggage, instead improvising with a headscarf. But I did always carry a candle and matches. Sometimes we must ignite our own hope.

So, this Christmas Eve, I set about dusting. Before getting stuck in, I set up a reward for my labours: I poured half a bottle of red wine into my jam kettle, dropped in some slices of orange and lemon studded with cloves, stirred it with a cinnamon stick and sprinkled on dried ginger. After I'd set it on top of the wood-burner to warm, with duster in hand, I began to work my way through the house. Every time I finished a room, I topped up my cheery hand-painted Spanish mug, chosen for its festive reds and greens. I didn't dare risk the heat of mulled wine in my favourite violet Bohemian crystal wine goblet, even though it would have looked spectacular.

No-one has a cottage quite like mine. They're all different in these parts, built to suit the whim and the budget of whoever was first to live in them. Nor does anyone have the same vast collection of souvenirs of globetrotting scattered about the house. In the days when I made my living mostly from travel journalism rather than book commissions and royalties, other hacks on the circuit were dismissive of my penchant for souvenir-hunting. They thought it made me less professional. They took home only items that could be bought from airport duty-free shops. There was a saying among them, massacring Samuel Johnson's famous dictum on London, that if a man was tired of duty free, he was tired of travel writing. Perhaps they were right. None of my immediate peers stayed the course in travel journalism, nor did they graduate into writing books. I was glad to separate myself from that pack as soon as I was able to pay my own way to wherever I wanted to write about.

I pitied their wives (in those days the hacks were mostly men) and their children, who might reasonably expect gifts from wherever their daddy had been on his latest facility visit – those thinly veiled bribes to write reports on hotels and resorts. Some of the men sneaked in last-minute gifts at the airport alongside the endless bottles of Calvados or ouzo or sake. Toblerones, the equivalent of fuel-station flowers in the gift stakes, don't count as thoughtful presents unless you're travelling from Switzerland.

I prided myself on never resorting to airport presents. The gifts I brought my parents, and later my nephew, then Sophie, were always carefully chosen from local craftsmen or women. Choosing Sophie's presents was fun – a Black Forest dirndl; wooden clogs in the right shoe size from Amsterdam; a traditional hand-painted wooden Swedish Dala horse, as unique as a fingerprint.

But I bought far more for myself than for anyone else.

'More to dust!' my mother would mutter at every new item I brought home. My parents' cottage was always my base, as I never had a permanent home abroad. In those days, Mother was the one who did the dusting. Now I must do it myself, I never mind. As I run the duster over each item, I admire it afresh, remembering with perfect clarity the moment and the place of acquisition. Some items need more delicate handling than others, such as an ornamental clamshell from Hong Kong, in whose open jaws lies a miniature carved landscape as creamy as the shell, complete with a lake, a river, a house and tiny Chinese people amid foliage daubed red and green. It's far too small for my duster, so I just blow it to dislodge any debris. Then the working water wheel dips into its painted river, spinning as if in a storm surge.

I can be as heavy handed as I like with my chunky wooden carvings from the Caribbean. As bright as tropical fish, they look out of place in the pallid English light, but I love them all the same. Polishing my cobalt wooden parrot, I feel Bahamian sunshine burnishing my face.

Other items have been thoughtfully fortified by their makers against careless cleaners, dipped in resin or drenched in varnish. It's ironic that someone felt the need to embed my piece of Berlin Wall in protective plastic. And yes, it is genuine. I was there when the Wall came down. I stayed on in the aftermath, helping enterprising souls from both sides to collect fragments of communist concrete, as in their enthusiasm they prised it apart with penknives, hammers, and bare hands.

'Good fences make good neighbours?' I murmured now, slipping the piece of Berlin Wall into my pocket. 'I don't think so.'

***

When I returned to the parlour, both the fire and the mulled wine were low. The heavy scent of spices and citrus hung in the air, melding with the sharp bite of pine. My hand slipped as I topped the jam kettle up from the rest of the bottle I'd left breathing on the hearth. I didn't mean to empty it, but why not?

I raised my next glass to the angel on top of the Christmas tree. Decades before, on a pavement in Durban, I'd watched a local boy, with skin as dark as the sun was bright, conjure up this concoction of red and white beads. Cleverly twisting them into shape on fine wire, he was so intent on his craft that he seemed oblivious to the seductive view of the Indian Ocean across the promenade. I wondered what had become of him.

Then my focus slid sideways from my South African angel to its backdrop. Night had fallen while I'd been dusting. I'd closed the upstairs shutters as I'd left each room, but not the ones downstairs. I've always liked the Dutch custom of leaving your front curtains or shutters open after lighting-up time to share the warmth of your home with passers-by. Now a very gentle rain was drifting slowly down behind my tree-top angel, turned into flecks of glitter by the streetlight across the road. Except the flecks were falling too slowly for rain.

Those sparkly flakes were very definitely snow.

On the radio, the carol service had long since finished, and now I caught a snatch of the weather forecast:

'In the south-west of England, all non-essential travel should be avoided.' There was a note of apology in the weatherman's voice. Perhaps he felt guilty at wrecking people's holiday plans. 'Treacherous conditions... warnings of ice...' I wondered whether he'd obey his own instructions.

Would Joshua have arrived safely at his nephew's? Stepping over to the window, I pulled aside just enough branches of my Christmas tree to peer beyond my front path and around to Joshua's garden. The pool of light on his frosty lawn told me he hadn't gone away after all. He was holed up in his parlour, same as me, with only his memories for company.

My proximity to the astringent scent of the pine needles was starting to make my eyes water, so I let the branches spring back into place. Then I opened the wood-burner to fling another log inside, refilled my Spanish mug, and settled down in my fireside chair to think.

***

In our childhood days, Billy had been notorious for playing Knock Down Ginger. In this silly, selfish game, youngsters think it the height of wit to rap at an innocent neighbour's door and run away. Then they hide, staying just close enough to witness their victim's puzzlement on opening the door to Mr Nobody. Did the latest generation of tearaways still play that game? I'd seen no evidence. Doubtless they're too busy playing with their electronic gadgets to find such foolishness entertaining.

So, I wondered whether, when Joshua heard a knock on his front door late on Christmas Eve, his first thought would be of Billy. Except Billy never left presents on people's doorsteps. Especially presents wrapped in vintage Egyptian newspaper.

Before Joshua could answer the knock, I darted back inside my house and closed my door as quietly as I could. The sharp trill of the telephone diverted me from ascertaining Joshua's reaction. As I picked up the receiver, I was still catching my breath.

'Merry Christmas Eve, Auntie May!' Sophie's sweet smile warmed her voice as she regaled me with the fun she and her friends were having in the snow. I was glad she didn't yet consider herself too old to build a snowman. Then she outlined the family's plans for Hogmanay. The New Year celebrations are so much more exciting in Scotland than they are south of the border in England, even if the revellers do need an extra public holiday on 2 January to get over them.

'She'll be writing to you in between times, May,' I heard her mother call in the background.

'I'll look forward to that, my dear,' I replied, though I knew full well that as the child was growing up, her letters were getting shorter and less frequent. Soon I'd be lucky to get so much as a postcard, but that's OK. Hadn't I done the same in response to Joshua's letters?

Sophie's father was next on the line. 'You will come as soon as you can, won't you, May?' Beneath his gruff voice, I could detect the plaintive plea of the little boy he'd once been. 'And you can stay as long as you like now that you're retired.'

'Yes, yes, of course, dear. Your delicious Highland air is just the tonic I need.'

And to see their dear faces, of course.

'I'm saving a drop of my best Highland whisky to share with you, May. But hang on, is that your doorbell?' He sounded miffed to have a rival for my attention. Frankly, I was as surprised as he was.

'Indeed it is. I had better attend to it. I'll call you tomorrow, dear. Merry Christmas.'

I set the receiver back in its cradle. As I made my way through to the hall, I steadied myself on the doorhandle. Through the small stained-glass window set into the front door, I could just make out a tall figure, slightly stooped.

My hands were shaking as I opened the door. To Joshua.

As he raised his cap and gave me a slight bow, a shy smile played beneath his still handsome moustache.

'Miss Sayers, may I wish you a merry Christmas?'

He didn't need to ask my permission. As I stepped back and motioned to him to come in, I saw that in his other hand, he was clutching the Egyptian newspaper in which I'd wrapped my symbolic gift to him: my piece of the fallen Berlin Wall. The package was no longer a flat slab, but chunky and round. At least he wasn't returning my gift unopened. But what had he wrapped in the paper for me?

He stamped the snow off his stout shoes and hung his cap on my hallstand before following me into the parlour, where he offered me the package. My hand dropped slightly as I took it. It was much heavier than it looked.

'I hear recycled wrapping paper is all the rage these days, May.' The familiar twinkle hadn't left his eyes. 'You may open it now. I won't make you wait until after church on Christmas morning.' Trying hard to sound casual, he seemed as nervous as I felt.

I sat down heavily in my fireside chair and set the package on my lap. Joshua remained standing in front of me.

I tried to contain my emotions as I peeled back the newspaper to reveal a lump of honey-coloured Cotswold stone, cold and rimy. When I gazed up at him for an explanation, he just smiled.

'The first of many stones I plan to remove to restore the dear old gate between our gardens.' His eyes locked onto mine. 'We can never go back to where we left off, May, but I believe it's not yet too late for us to harvest a little more precious time together. I do hope you agree.'

I clapped my hand to my mouth, covering a smile broad enough to hurt my cheeks. I don't know why I, the unshockable seasoned traveller, said what I said next:

'Well yes, of course, but whatever will the neighbours think?'

Joshua threw back his head and laughed, slapping his tweed-covered thighs.

'Oh, my dear May, does it really matter what anyone else thinks? Just allow me to assure you that your closest neighbour –' he tapped his chest '– deems your consent cause for celebration.' He pulled a small glass flask of sloe gin from the sagging pocket of his trousers. 'And tomorrow, let's spend Christmas Day together. The first of many special days that we might share.'

As I nodded, loneliness slid from my shoulders like the snow from an Alpine chalet roof. I set his stone gently on the hearth, where it still lies today.

When he reached out his hands to pull me up from my armchair to face him, I wished I'd bought some of Billy's mistletoe after all.

Wild Bells

'But I wanted to spend New Year's Eve alone with you,' I protested. 'That's why we came back from Mum and Dad's so soon.'

It was my second Christmas with – or without – Hector. The first Christmas after we'd got together, I'd travelled to Inverness to stay with my parents from Christmas Eve until the second of January, so I could celebrate Hogmanay too. This year, we'd spent Christmas in the village, but bagged a cheap flight to Inverness for a couple of days with my parents. The difference in the weather and the daylight hours in Scotland was remarkable. While I was sad to say goodbye to my parents, it was a relief to return to the longer, milder, drier days of the Cotswold winter.

After all that dashing about, I was looking forward now to seeing in the New Year at home in Wendlebury Barrow with Hector. So, I was not best pleased when Hector announced on the thirtieth of December that he'd chosen to see in the New Year with seven other people instead of me.

Why seven? Because there are eight bells in the tower of the parish church of St Bride, and several of the Wendlebury Ringers were laid low by winter bugs, leaving them one person short. To be fair, it's not quite true to say Hector chose them over me. Rather, our vicar, the Reverend Gerard Murray, had cajoled him into volunteering.

'Couldn't they just ring seven bells instead?' I asked as I set down a cup of hot chocolate in front of the vicar at his table in the tearoom. 'Seven is still a lot of bells. Besides, isn't that a thing? They talk about ringing seven bells, don't they?'

Hector, stickering Christmas books with discounted prices for our January sale, gave a snort of laughter.

'You mean knock seven bells out of someone? That's nothing to do with bell ringing. It's a naval term, referring to the eight bells of a watch. Knocking seven bells out of someone means very nearly finishing them off in a fight. Rest assured, sweetheart, no-one in this village will be doing that to anyone on New Year's Eve.'

'I'm pleased to hear it,' I replied, though it was small comfort for the problem at hand.

The vicar warmed his pale hands on his mug of cocoa. His fingertips were blue with cold after he'd trudged up and down the high street to deliver the January issue of the *Wendlebury Parish News*, his usual team of distributors immobilised by illness.

'Hector's right, Sophie.' His watery eyes twinkled. 'That's a seafaring reference. He'll be rather more safe in a bell tower.'

I refused to be mollified even by dear, kind Reverend Murray.

'That's not what I've heard. Carol told me once that there are loads of ways you can come to a sticky end in a bell tower, even without touching a bell or a bell-rope. Take the spiral staircase for starters.' I've never liked spiral staircases. They make me dizzy. 'Carol said the stone steps have been worn so crooked by a thousand years of footfall that they're an accident waiting to happen.'

Sitting at the next table, old Billy slammed his empty coffee cup onto its saucer, startling everyone in the previously peaceful shop.

'If it's accidents waiting to happen that you're looking for, you want to go to the top of the church tower and out onto the balustrade. Paul Taylor, now –'

'No need to bring that up, Bill,' the vicar cut in hastily. 'But as our longest serving ringer, perhaps you'd care to explain to Sophie why we need all eight bells to be rung tomorrow night.'

Billy raised his unruly white eyebrows at me as I crossed the room to the trade counter.

'Who's Paul Taylor?' I whispered to Hector, confident that Billy was too deaf to hear.

'I'll tell you later,' he replied in a low voice.

'She don't need me to tell her why we need eight bells,' retorted Billy. 'She's a piano player.'

'What's the piano got to do with it?' I was genuinely puzzled. 'Do you mean they're both percussion instruments?' To be honest, I'd never even thought of church bells as a musical instrument until he'd said that. That made gruff, grumpy Billy a musician. I saw him in a whole new light.

Billy tutted at my ignorance. 'I've heard you making those poor kiddies you teach bash out their scales upstairs.'

Since Hector had installed his parents' upright in the flat above the shop, I'd added piano lessons to the services we offer as part of the Hector's House business, having passed my Grade 8 with Distinction while still at school.

'Wouldn't you think they hadn't completed the job if they stopped at the seventh note?'

'I suppose so,' I demurred, going over to collect his empty cup for a refill.

The vicar picked up his teaspoon to stir the Christmas tree of cocoa dust into his mocha.

'Billy's being a little disingenuous,' he put in. 'There are plenty of times we've had fewer than eight ringers in action, and many towers have a different number of bells, whether fewer, such as four or six, or more, such as ten or even twelve. We don't really have to ring all eight every time just because we have eight bells. For example, on sombre occasions such as Remembrance Day, we might ring the minor five – that's bells two to six – to create a more mournful sound. But the departure of the old year and arrival of the new one should be a joyful occasion, so we'd plan to ring all eight to celebrate. If we rang with fewer, those ringers lying in their sick beds just now would feel they'd let the band down by staying away.'

Band. So bell ringers counted as a band. That was news to me too. Suddenly they were starting to sound almost rock'n'roll.

'Of course, they all live within hearing distance of the bells,' the vicar added. Everyone in Wendlebury Barrow couldn't help but hear them, as the church lies at the heart of the village. 'And when we have such an accomplished ringer as Hector all hale and hearty, it would seem a shame to disappoint them.'

I almost dropped the jug I was holding beneath the steam nozzle.

'An accomplished ringer? Hector?' I stared at him in puzzlement. 'I didn't know he was any kind of ringer.' I set down the jug that was now brimming with frothy hot milk. 'Except a dead ringer for his brother Horace, of course.'

When I was the only one to laugh at my joke, I realised that since Hector and Horace had been born and raised in Wendlebury, thirty years on, any jest about the identical twins must have been told too many times to be funny.

The vicar smiled politely. 'Allow me to enlighten you, my dear. In their youth, both Hector and Horace were a fine pair of bell ringers.'

'Oi, I'm not old yet!' cried Hector.

The vicar, at least twice his age, continued. 'They took to it like naturals from the moment their father first brought them to ringing practice night. They were still at the village school then, just ten years old. Isn't that so, Hector?'

Hector gave a nostalgic grin.

'We had to stand on boxes to learn the ropes at first,' he chimed in.

'Before long, they were ringing competently alongside the grown-ups,' said the vicar. 'Their father was proud of how quickly they picked up the technique. Learning to control the bell is a fine art, especially when you're a skinny young lad without a man's bodily strength. You can't ring in sequence with others until you've learned the basics of bell control.'

I poured the milk into Billy's coffee cup and dusted another Christmas tree through the metal template.

'Really? I had no idea it was that nuanced. I thought you just took it in turns to pull on the ropes.'

I'd seen the ringers in action many times from ground level, but never been up to the ringing chamber to see them close at hand.

Billy chortled as he scooped up the cocoa dust Christmas tree and slurped it off his teaspoon.

'You're not the first and you won't be the last to assume bell ringing is as easy as pulling the chain.'

'Chain? I thought you used ropes.' The corners of his mouth twitched upwards as he waited for me to catch his meaning. 'Oh, you mean like pulling a chain in an old-fashioned toilet.' Not that there were many of those about these days, but I was willing to bet Billy's bathroom still boasted an overhead cistern. His old cottage hadn't been modernised since his mother had died.

The mental image of the ringers lined up as synchronised flushers in an old public toilet made us all laugh out loud. I didn't like to admit that was how I really had thought the bells worked.

The vicar produced a small leather-bound jotter from his inside jacket pocket and turned to a clean sheet. I passed him the pencil from my order pad, and he sketched an upside-down bell inside a circle. His drawing reminded me of Leonardo da Vinci's famous sketch of an encircled man with limbs outstretched. The clapper was resting on one side of the bell's mouth. At the pointy end of the bell, he added a line that led to the perimeter of the circle, and then around it, with the end hanging down to a hastily drawn stick man whose arms were raised to grasp it.

'Billy's colourful analogy is not far off for countries where the rope is simply suspended from the top of the bell, but in this country, we do full-circle ringing. The bell's mounted within a wheel, and the rope turns it 360 degrees, until the clapper strikes the side of the bell. It strikes alternate sides as the wheel turns full circle at every pull of the rope. With sufficient practice, you gain control of how quickly or slowly the wheel turns, and thus can time the stroke. Accomplished teams will be able to space the strokes precisely in specific sequences, just as you depress the keys on your piano to play a tune.'

'Except bells don't play tunes,' added Billy. 'We ring rounds or changes or peals. Rounds sound the bells in order, change ringing swaps their order, and peals mean there's a swap in every round.'

I blinked as I tried to process this intelligence.

'As twins, Hector and Horace were on the same wavelength,' said the vicar. 'Almost to the point of telepathy, so it came naturally to them to keep in perfect time with each other. Ringing in sequence with six fellow band members was not such a huge step as it might have been for other beginners, especially when those other six were very skilful.'

Billy cleared his throat. The vicar took the hint.

'Billy is our longest-standing ringer these days, though Ian is Tower Captain as he is happier doing the requisite admin.'

'Still leaves us one ringer short for tomorrow night, though.' Billy sighed. 'Where's Horace when you need him?'

That was a rhetorical question. Everyone in the village knew that for the last few years, Horace had been living in Australia, where he worked as a tour guide in the outback. Of the Munro twins, he's by far the more daring, having survived a near-fatal childhood illness that left him feeling immortal and Hector cautious.

'Sorry, Billy, but he didn't come home for Christmas this year,' said Hector.

'Most kind of you to volunteer, then, Hector,' said the vicar. 'So as long as no-one else falls sick by tomorrow night, we'll have our eight after all.'

Between them, they'd made it impossible for him to refuse. Hector mouthed 'sorry' to me behind the vicar's back. But I was determined somehow to spend New Year in the bell tower with them.

***

'If you must go, can I come too?' I suggested to Hector as we were shutting up the shop later.

'I'm guessing from our earlier conversation that you've never rung a bell yourself before?'

'Spot on.'

'Then I'm afraid tomorrow night's not the time for you to start. As the vicar said, you need experience to be able to ring in sequence with the rest of the band. In untrained hands, a bell rope can be dangerous.

For example, I once saw a rope fly out of a novice's hands and loop itself around their neck.'

I shuddered. 'Did it strangle them?'

'No, thanks to the lightning reflexes of Joshua, who whisked it away and brought the rope and the bell back under control.'

I stopped wiping the table and stared in astonishment. 'Joshua? My Joshua?'

My elderly next-door-neighbour Joshua moved so slowly that he couldn't have stopped a tortoise in the road. It's easy to forget people you've only known as old and frail were once young and vigorous.

'Oh yes, Joshua was Tower Captain when Horace and I were learning to ring. He was an excellent and patient teacher. He only gave up when he became too unsteady to climb the stairs to the ringing chamber. Dreadful shame. It must have left a huge gap in his life. It's not just the ringing that's good fun, it's the camaraderie – the satisfaction of effective teamwork, producing something together that none of you could manage alone.'

I rinsed the cloth in the sink, wrung it out and hung it on the rail to dry.

'Yes, I can see that. Poor Joshua.'

'Fortunately, not long after that, your Auntie May retired to the village and provided him with an alternative occupation. They certainly made the most of the time they had left together.'

I smiled at the mental image of the childhood sweethearts rekindling their romance in old age.

'If I can't ring, is there something else I could do to help?' I hated to resort to stereotyping, but given my day job in the tearoom, I grasped at an obvious solution. 'Maybe I could serve you all drinks? I'm guessing bell ringing is thirsty work.'

Hector pulled the drawer from the till and began to cash up.

'That's a kind thought, Sophie, and in the olden days, bell ringers were famous for their capacity for beer. Ringing contests were sponsored by pubs, with liquid prizes. But there'll be no time to stop for refreshments tomorrow night. We'll only ring for half an hour from midnight onwards, so as not to disturb light sleepers. But here's a thought.'

He lifted the flap in the trade counter and passed through the gap, heading for the poetry section. Taking a volume of Tennyson from the shelf, he turned to the index, then flicked through to his chosen page.

'You could read this to us a few minutes before midnight, before we start to ring. That would add an extra something to the occasion.'

He brought the book over to show me and opened it at *Ring Out, Wild Bells*.

I brightened.

'Yes, yes, I'd love to. If the others don't mind.'

'I'm sure they'd love it, if you practise enough to get the timing right. You must finish a minute or two before midnight strikes, so that you don't delay the ringing.'

***

On New Year's Eve, we didn't need to be at St Bride's until 11.30pm, so after a fortifying tea of beef casserole with dumplings, we joined what seemed like half the adults of the village at The Bluebird, where the atmosphere was warm and lively. For the first little while, we circulated among the bustling crowd, catching up with friends and neighbours about how we'd spent our Christmases.

'Another pint, Hector?' I asked, as we finally found a couple of free chairs at a table occupied by members of the Wendlebury Writers' group, some of the first friends I'd made when I moved to the village two summers before.

Hector drained his near-empty tankard before setting it down on the table.

'Better not. I must keep a relatively clear head for ringing shortly, especially when I haven't rung for so long.'

'How long has it been?' I asked him.

He looked away. 'Since a couple of weeks after you arrived in the village. I didn't want you to think I was an old fuddy-duddy.'

I snorted. 'You idiot, Hector. I'd never have thought that. I'd have been impressed.'

'You might not be if I've lost my touch.'

Just then, Billy staggered up and laid a paternal hand on Hector's shoulder.

'Don't you worry, boy. Bell ringing is like riding a bicycle. It'll come back to you in no time the minute you gets your hands on that sally.'

My eyes widened in alarm. 'Who's Sally?' I pictured some floozy as the real attraction of ringing to the gaggle of men due in the tower in the next half hour.

To my consternation, both Hector and Billy fell about laughing.

'Sally ain't no lady,' chortled Billy, casting Hector a conspiratorial look.

'All the nice boys love a sally,' replied Hector, wiping a tear from his eye.

Their raucous exchange caught the attention of Ian, who was sitting with a cluster of friends at the next table. He leaned towards me with a kindly smile.

'They're winding you up, love. The sally is the fluffy material attached to the bell rope, a metre or so from the end of the tail. It's to stop you getting burns when you catch the moving rope.'

Yet another potential source of injury for bell ringers. I wondered whether they kept a first-aid box in the ringing chamber.

While Billy and Hector continued their banter about 'bits of fluff', I thanked Ian for his explanation.

'Will you be ringing tonight?'

Ian got to his feet and straightened his back, standing tall.

'Wouldn't miss it. I've rung every New Year in since 1983, and it wouldn't feel right I wasn't up St Bride's Tower when midnight chimed. So, sup up, lads, and look lively. The vicar will be there with the key any minute to open up.'

I drained the last mouthful of my Sav Blanc.

'You mean the church has been locked today?'

Like most remote country churches, St Bride's was kept locked for security in the winter months, when tourist traffic was low, but for the twelve days of Christmas, the vicar liked to keep it open for anyone who sought a quiet, safe retreat from the hubbub of modern commercial celebrations. He also invited villagers to go in to light candles for 'those who we see no more', as he put it. I'd been in myself on Christmas Eve to light a candle for Auntie May.

'Oh no, the church has been open all day, but the bell tower's kept locked when the ringers aren't in it,' said Ian. 'The spiral staircase, the ringing chamber, and the bell loft above are too hazardous to allow the public to wander about up there unsupervised.

As caretaker at the village school, he had a raised awareness of health and safety risks, which might have been another reason he was Tower Captain.

'Not to mention the balustrade, open to the elements, at the top of the tower,' put in Billy, his previously playful demeanour now vanished.

'Yes, *not* to mention it, please, Billy,' echoed Ian. He set his empty tankard on the table and clapped his hands together. 'OK, ringers, let's be having you.'

To my surprise, it wasn't only Billy and Hector that got to their feet, but two of the ladies from the writers' group, as well as Ian's mate Stephen Clements. Suddenly, I understood why his nickname in the village was Saint – as in the old children's rhyme *Oranges and Lemons*.

I stood up too.

'I didn't know you were a ringer, Sophie,' said Saint, pleasantly. A slight, shortish man in his forties, he was dwarfed by Ian's tall, stocky frame. I was glad to see proof that brute strength wasn't a prerequisite to ring bells. Maybe I'd try my hand at it in the New Year and encourage Hector to take it up again. I like to learn something new each year. In the one about to depart, I'd taken up knitting.

'Not yet, Saint, I'm just coming to watch – and to read a poem, if everyone's happy with that? Tennyson's *Ring Out, Wild Bells*.'

'Great idea, Sophie. Thanks.'

As we strolled in a little huddle up the high street to the church, mild drizzle twinkled beneath the soft yellow rays of the streetlights. As ever, I enjoyed gazing at all the cottages along the way, admiring the Christmas trees and fairy lights in their windows and front gardens. There were none of the brash model Santas or illuminated inflatable snowmen that you find in city gardens at this time of year. In Wendlebury, there is an unwritten agreement to keep outdoor Christmas decorations traditional, almost as if they'd just sprung from the earth ahead of the early spring bulbs now poking their buds above the chilly dark-brown soil. A few people had left their curtains open to see in the New Year. Come Twelfth Night, when they all took down their decorations and closed their curtains and shutters against the long, cold winter nights, it would seem so very dark.

On almost every front door hung a wreath, much of their foliage sourced from the evergreens in the residents' own back gardens or from Billy's door-to-door deliveries in early December, assisted by his teenage sidekick Tommy, of holly, ivy and mistletoe gathered from local woodland. Some of the wreaths were adorned with scarlet ribbons. The occasional swathe of tartan made me miss my parents and picture what they might be doing now, in their big old granite house on the banks of the dark River Ness. I decided to light a candle at St Bride's for them as soon as the ringing had finished.

When we arrived at St Bride's, the great west door stood ajar, a sliver of yellow light luring us into the vestry. As we pushed the ancient door open, the vicar was walking towards us down the aisle, with Tommy at his side. In the darkness behind them, dots of yellow light flickered like stars, but at chest height, and I realised they must have been lighting a few candles. I knew Tommy missed his father, who had abandoned the family when he was little and his sister Sina smaller still. Perhaps the vicar had encouraged him to light a candle for his absent dad, while also lighting some of his own. It's easy to forget sometimes that the vicar, source of so much condolence, comfort, and hope to others at times of distress and bereavement, must have had losses of his own.

'Go on up, my dears, I've already opened the tower for you, and I've turned on the lights in the ringing chamber.'

Tommy scampered ahead, bounding up the deeply pitted stone stairs with the spring-loaded grace and confidence of a cat. The others in our party followed, with me lingering to be second to last. Hector, chivalrous as ever, stood back, allowing me to go before him, aware of my nervousness.

'Don't worry, I'll provide a soft landing if you fall,' he reassured me.

I planted my feet carefully where over the centuries the tread of hundreds of villagers had worn grooves into the steps. I could literally feel their presence. Disconcerted to find the staircase too narrow to allow a handrail, I was grateful for the rope suspended down the centre of the spiral, despite the cobwebs, and I hung on to it with both hands. Even so, my ascent was unsteady, and I was conscious of picking up pale stone dust on my coat from the outer wall as I climbed.

At the twenty-third step, a smaller version of the west porch door – pitch-dark oak planks joined together by black iron straps – stood open to the ringing chamber. The lively chatter of the ringers was constrained by the stone walls of the small room, adding to the cosy feel of this patch of bright light high above the dark body of the empty church. The platform was overlooked by the great rose window above the west end door on one side. Opposite the window was chest-high panelling topped by an iron rail embedded at either end in the ancient stone. Above the rail, the platform was open to the church. From the nave, the ringing chamber reminded me of a medieval minstrels' gallery, and now I realised that from the ringers' vantage point, they had the best view in the house.

I gazed up to the next part of the spiral staircase, winding into infinite blackness beyond. I was very grateful to step through into the bright and cheery ringing chamber, and have Hector close the door on the dark void above us.

Despite the air being so cold that we could see our breaths as we exhaled, the ringers immediately divested themselves of their coats and hats and hung them on the wall-mounted coat rack. I guessed ringing would warm them up in no time. I kept my outdoor things on and went to stand in the centre of the chamber, wondering where the best place for me would be to read the poem.

'Mind the spider, girlie!' cried Billy, and I jumped back, glancing anxiously about me. I knew a colony of bats lived at the top of the tower, but hadn't given any thought to any other wildlife that might have made their homes here. I brushed randomly at my hair, thinking it would have been too easy for a spider to alight on me as I climbed the dusty staircase.

'Right above your head!' shrieked Tommy, gleefully.

Hector grabbed me by the shoulders and pulled me back towards the perimeter wall. I glanced upwards – a huge eight-legged metal contraption descended on a thick cord, suspended from the centre of the ceiling like an evil chandelier. The cord then ran along the ceiling, through a few iron hooks to hold it in place, and down the far corner of the wall to a pulley system. At shoulder height, Ian was winding a handle to spool out the cord until the metal 'spider' was just a metre off the floor.

Looped over each of the eight metal legs were the lower ends of the bell ropes. The other ends of the ropes ran through eight neat holes in the ceiling to the bells above.

Hector clasped his arms protectively about my waist, and I leaned back against him, my heart still pounding after the alert.

'Biggest spider you've ever seen, eh, sweetheart?' My shoulders went limp as the adrenaline dispersed. 'It's what we call the device that keeps the ropes tidy and out of people's reach when we're not ringing.'

'I knew that,' I lied, and he gave me a reassuring squeeze, knowing that I hadn't.

But there was no time to lose. Each ringer unhooked a rope from the spider and tied the lower end into a loose knot to keep it clear of the floor. Then Ian cranked the spider back up to the ceiling and locked it into place.

'That must be the sally,' I said to Hector, reaching out to run my fingertips over the blue-and-white-striped sausage of fluffy material that encased each thick hemp rope a metre or so from the loop at the bottom end. Hector startled me by grabbing my hand and snatching it away behind my back. My nerves jangled again.

'No touching the ropes!' he barked, but when he saw my hurt expression, his manner softened. 'Sorry, sweetheart, I didn't mean to snap. It's just that the bells can be dangerous in untrained hands. Look, why don't you make yourself comfortable on the ledge there and settle down to watch us, once you've read your poem. I think you'll find it interesting.'

He indicated the broad, deep, low windowsill beneath the stained-glass rose window that in summer caught the sunshine's rays, dappling the floor of the nave red and blue. The huge slabs of hand-cut Cotswold stone, long ago chiselled smooth by medieval craftsmen, would have been chilly to sit on, so someone had laid a vast tapestry cushion, an elongated version of the kneelers in the pews below. A neat row of eight bells had been worked in bronze coloured wool thread against an azure background, with a saint's name lettered beneath: Mary, Bridget, Catherine, Francis, Matthew, Mark, Luke, and John. In the corner were initials that I recognised to be Carol's – so she must have been the dedicated needlewoman to create this thoughtful addition, presumably to mark the turn of the millennium as she'd added the year 2000. It must have taken ages, but it still looked like new – it had worn well. I made a mental note to express my appreciation next time I saw her.

'Look out, Billy, there's blood on your rope!' cried Mary.

I drew a sharp intake of breath. 'Oh my goodness, that sounds like a sinister book title, *Blood on the Rope*. Has there been foul play?'

Billy looked down at his left thumb and wiped it on the seat of his baggy corduroy trousers.

'It's only my blood,' he said. 'Scratched it on a bit of my holly wreath earlier. When you're on blood thinners like I am, you bleed at the drop of a hat. Takes ages to heal over.'

That was a relief.

'Sophie's going to read us a poem to get us all in the mood,' Ian was saying. 'Do you know, in all the years I've been ringing, we've never started with a poem to ring the New Year in, but I think it's a great idea. Who knows, Sophie, you may even have started a new tradition?'

In a village so steeped in customary ways of doing things, I was excited and flattered to think I might be contributing to those ways for evermore.

'Thank you, Ian.' I suddenly felt shy, even though I knew him well from our work together on the pantomime that I'd written the previous year for the Wendlebury Players, of which Ian was a keen member.

'But before you do that, Sophie, let's get these bells up,' he added.

I followed the line of the ropes to the neat, square holes in the wooden ceiling.

'Aren't the bells up there already?' From the deep, rich sounds that resounded throughout the village every Sunday and on practice night, I assumed they must be enormous. Surely they were far too big for the ringers to take out from wherever they were kept in between times – a cupboard in the vestry, perhaps – whenever they wanted to ring them?

The whole band burst out laughing. Mary was the first to pull herself together.

'Don't worry, Sophie, the bells are already up there in the tower, above our heads.'

Instinctively I ducked, fearful of a heavy bell falling through the floorboards. At least I'd be safer on my window seat than standing in the circle of ringers immediately beneath the bells – not so poor Hector.

Mary held up one hand, curling her fingers around in the shape of a bell with its mouth facing the floor.

'What Ian means,' she continued, 'is that we need to raise the bells. Between ringing, they're left with the mouths facing downwards, as they're safer that way. Before we can ring them, we must raise their mouths heavenwards.' She inverted her cupped hand. 'So, now we have to stand them upright, ready for full-circle ringing.'

'Go for it, ringers!' cried Ian, and suddenly, the little gang who had been standing idly was hard at work. First, they coiled the tail of their rope in one hand, as far up as the bottom of the sally, and then they hauled on the sally energetically with both hands, putting their backs into the effort. They held on to the other end of the rope as the sally rebounded, gradually spooling out the coil with each pull, until they were alternating steadily between heaving on the sally, letting the rope rise until the sally almost touched the ceiling, and hoicking down the tail end to bring the sally back into their grasp. The speed with which the rope plied up and down made me realise how heavy the bells were, their weight fighting back against the ringers' efforts.

No wonder they'd taken off their coats already. It was clearly warm work.

The bells were clanging raucously together now, with no apparent thought given to order or pattern. So much for Billy's scales. Gradually, they fell silent, the smaller bells first – I guessed it took less effort to raise those than the big ones. Their coils of rope had gone, and the sally was motionless in the bell ringers' hands, quivering only slightly as the reverberations of the clanging bells died away. They knotted the tails of the ropes again, and stood back silently, some mopping their brows, others taking a swift swig of something from a flask or bottle produced from their pockets, and all breathing a little faster.

I realised now that the order in which the ringers were standing was not as random as it had at first seemed. The ladies took the lighter bells and the men the heavier, with Tommy in between on the fourth. Ian, by the far the sturdiest of the men, was on the tenor – the biggest bell with the deepest tone – and Mary was on the smallest, known as the treble. I'd worked out those names by studying the peal boards on the walls – the gilt-lettered wooden panels that commemorated when particularly long, complex sequences had been rung on special occasions, such as the millennium and for coronations, not only of King Charles III, but of Queen Elizabeth II and her predecessors going back to the early nineteenth century. Edward VIII was conspicuous by his absence. Those peals had all taken three hours or more. I was relieved that the bell ringers had made the decision not to ring a peal tonight.

'That's the bells up,' Stephen told me. 'They're ready to ring whenever we like now.'

Ian glanced at the wall clock – a cheap plastic one that was a poor imitation of the grand gold-painted clock-face on the outside of the tower. 'It's coming up to five to twelve now, so there's just time for you to read your poem before it strikes midnight, Sophie. Why don't you stand up so you can project better?' All his years in the Wendlebury Players were not wasted. 'Then sit back down as soon as you're done and stay sitting until I tell the ringers to stand in half an hour's time.'

That surprised me. 'You mean you only stand up when you've finished ringing?' If they sat on the floor, surely the ringers wouldn't even be able to reach the ends of their ropes, never mind the fluffy sallies.

Ian bit back a smile. 'In bell ringing, stand means stop ringing.' He held up his palm, straight-armed, as he did to the traffic when on duty as a lollipop man. 'It refers to setting your bell to stand at the top of the full circle, holding it against the stay.'

'Ah,' I said, trying to sound sage. It was an awful lot to take in. I was beginning to wonder whether I'd ever make sense of the whole business. There was more to this bell ringing malarkey than I'd thought possible.

I got to my feet and pulled the poetry book out of my handbag. As I took a deep breath, ready to begin, I gazed into the distance at the flickering dots of light in front of the altar, mirrored now and again in the silver cross and brassware like a silent, respectful firework display.

I cleared my throat, self-conscious in the silence that had settled in the wake of the mighty clangour. As I opened my mouth to read the first word, I tried to shut out the distant creaks and squeaks, perhaps the sounds of an old building settling down for the night as the temperature outside continued to fall. Eight pairs of eyes rested upon me – nine, actually, as the vicar had pushed open the door and crept across the floor to sit on the window seat behind me.

I began to read Tennyson's immortal lines:

Ring out, wild bells, to the wild sky,
The flying cloud, the frosty light:
The year is dying in the night;
Ring out, wild bells, and let him die.

Ring out the old, ring in the new,
Ring, happy bells, across the snow:
The year is going, let him go;
Ring out the false, ring in the true.

Ring out the grief that saps the mind
*   For those that here we see no more;*
*   Ring out the feud of rich and poor,*
*   Ring in redress to all mankind.*

Ring out a slowly dying cause,
*   And ancient forms of party strife;*
*   Ring in the nobler modes of life,*
*   With sweeter manners, purer laws.*

Ring out the want, the care, the sin,
*   The faithless coldness of the times;*
*   Ring out, ring out my mournful rhymes*
*   But ring the fuller minstrel in.*

Ring out false pride in place and blood,
*   The civic slander and the spite;*
*   Ring in the love of truth and right,*
*   Ring in the common love of good.*

Ring out old shapes of foul disease;
*   Ring out the narrowing lust of gold;*
*   Ring out the thousand wars of old,*
*   Ring in the thousand years of peace.*

Ring in the valiant man and free,
*   The larger heart, the kindlier hand;*
*   Ring out the darkness of the land,*
*   Ring in the Christ that is to be.*

There was a moment's silence as my last word died away, then to my surprise, the ringers broke out in a spontaneous round of applause. Then, as Ian glanced at the clock, they untied their ropes, draped the tail ends across their left palms, and reached with both hands to grasp the centre of the sallies. As one, they looked at Ian, who had his eyes on the clock.

I had just leaned back in anticipation of the inevitable flurry of activity, crossing my arms and legs, when the vicar laid a hand on my knee. I drew back in astonishment.

'Never cross your legs in a bell tower,' he advised, immediately withdrawing his hand. His gesture had been purely instructive, rather than flirtatious.

'Why not? Is it bad luck, like whistling on board ship?'

He smiled. 'Just a practical precaution, my dear. You don't want to trip up a ringer or, worse still, get your foot caught in the loop at the tail end of a rope, and find yourself hoisted aloft by the ankle.'

I uncrossed my legs immediately and planted both feet firmly on the ground, not wanting to end up like a wild animal swinging from a tree in the forest.

A metallic click and a whirr above our heads told us the church clock was about to strike the midnight hour. I sensed every ringer tense their muscles, like cats preparing to pounce.

'Everybody ready?' cried Mary on the smallest bell. 'Look to! Treble's going. She's gone.'

She immediately gave her rope a vigorous tug, and the other seven ringers, at perfectly spaced intervals, copied her action. An immaculate downward scale rang out as the church clock struck midnight.

I stared at the ceiling, almost hypnotised by the ropes as they rose and fell over and over again. Every Sunday and practice night since I'd moved to Wendlebury, I'd heard the bells ring, but always from ground level, whether inside or outside the church.

'I'd expected the sound to be louder up here in the ringing chamber, where we are so much closer to the bells,' I said to the vicar, raising my voice to be heard.

'As long as you steer clear of the bell loft, you are all right,' he replied. 'It's astonishing how much the floorboards muffle and mellow the sound, but if you were stand right next to the bells in full swing, you'd be driven insane or deaf, or both.'

'That's hard to imagine from here, where the sound is so soothing. The steady repetitions make me feel quite meditational.'

A sharp shout from Ian interrupted my elegy. 'Three over two!'

I must have looked baffled, again.

'That means bells three and two change places,' the vicar explained. That made sense. I realised Dinah, ringing the third bell, had turned from watching Jacky, on the second bell, to following Mary on the first. 'You've heard of ringing the changes? That's what they're doing now: change-ringing.'

'Five over four!' cried Ian, and after a few more repetitions, 'Seven over six!'

The bells settled into a new order, and the vicar said, 'That pattern's called Queens. All the different patterns have names.'

As they rang, I noticed how each ringer's technique varied. Some watched the rope of the bell they had to follow; others stared as if unseeing into the centre of the circle. Either they were ringing by ear rather than by sight, or they were watching the rope they were following out of the corner of their eye.

All but Tommy pulled at their rope with an economical, steady action, barely moving any part of their body except their arms and shoulders, reminding me of old-fashioned automaton toys. Tommy seemed to be giving it a lot more welly, bending from the waist, and expending far more energy than the others. Sometimes he even let the rope lift him slightly off the ground, earning him a reproving stare from Ian. I guessed his slender, boyish frame required far greater effort than that of the adults. Ian, meanwhile, continued to call out pairs of numbers as the ringers nimbly swapped places to vary the sound sequence, now and again shouting 'Go rounds!' to return them to a descending scale.

Despite the distraction value of Tommy's frantic capers, my gaze settled upon Hector. Billy had been right. Hector was ringing on autopilot, as if he'd been doing it for decades, his motion steady and assured as his strong arms rose above his head and fell again, keeping his rope taut and under control. He didn't need to watch the other ringers to know when to haul on the rope. I could almost have believed that the rope was ringing him. His animal grace was a joy to watch, and I would happily have spectated for longer, but all too soon the allotted half hour was up.

'Down in rounds!' barked Ian, and the downward scale speeded up as the ringers let the ropes slacken, coiling them in again as the notes blurred and blended into each other. Suddenly, they all dropped the coils and the tails of the long ropes fell to the floor, leaving the ringers hanging onto the sallies, this time chiming the bells in sequence with each tug.

'Three, two, one, stand!' cried Ian, and the bells fell silent all at once.

He cranked the spider down from the ceiling, and the ringers looped their ropes neatly onto its legs. When he raised it up again, it was hard to believe these neat, tidy ropes had just been the cause of so much sound. Then the band began to slap each other on the back and shake hands, and to produce from their pockets various bottles and flasks to raise New Year toasts to each other.

'My best damson gin, this is,' boasted Stephen Clements. 'Took first prize at the Village Show last summer, and I've been saving it specially for tonight.'

'Can't beat sloe gin if you ask me,' said Billy, pulling a small screw-top jam-jar filled with a viscous maroon liquor from his baggy trouser pocket.

'Another energy drink for me,' declared Tommy, pulling a slender, garish tin from his jeans pocket. 'My fifth tonight.'

'No!' we all cried in unison as he slipped his finger under the ring pull, anticipating an explosion after all his jigging about.

Just then the door burst open. A small, dishevelled figure in a dusty navy duffle coat and squashy brown felt hat almost fell into the ringing chamber and staggered across the hessian carpet towards Tommy.

'Oh, my goodness, it's the ghost of Paddington Bear!' I cried, and everyone laughed.

Then the hat fell off to reveal the tousled curls of Tommy's little sister.

'Sina! What are you doing here? Mum'll go ape if she knows you're out of bed.'

'Well, she won't know, will she?' retorted Sina, folding her arms and squaring up to her big brother. Thankfully, her arrival had distracted him from opening his drink can. 'She's still in the pub. Special licence on New Year's Eve, isn't there, and then probably a lock-in. I just followed you from home and hid among the choir's robes in the vestry while you and the vicar were setting things on fire down at the front there. Then I sneaked up to the top of the tower to wait till you'd finished ringing.'

Ian covered his face with his hands.

'Sina, promise me you will never, ever go up beyond the ringing chamber again,' he instructed her. 'And never, under any circumstances, go into the bell loft or onto the balustrade.'

'Do you think I'm stupid?' she retorted. 'After I heard you all go into the ringing chamber, I left the bell loft and played on the stairs. I invented a whole new game. It's a bit like hopscotch.'

In my mind's eye, I pictured her being crushed by a swinging bell or tumbling headfirst down the stairs. But, as ever, Sina was undaunted and unscathed.

'I don't see why I should be the only one in the family to be in bed at midnight. Happy New Year, Tommy, by the way. I wanted to be the first to say it you.' Tommy's lips twitched with pleasure at his sister's rare public show of affection. 'No-one else has said it to you yet, have they?'

'No,' Tommy lied, crossing his fingers behind his back. 'Happy New Year, Sina.'

He held out his arms, and in her haste to hug him, she fell into them, tripping over her wellies. He caught her before she could hit the ground. As they hugged, the back of her duffle coat rode up slightly, revealing her Winnie-the-Pooh pyjamas.

'Don't tell Mum on her, will you, everybody?' he urged, peering over her shoulder. 'I'll see her safe home now and into bed before Mum gets back from the pub.'

We gave him our word. Then everyone crowded around to take our turn at wishing them both their best New Year yet.

As we eventually gravitated towards the staircase, shrugging on our coats, wrapping scarves round our necks, and tugging on gloves and hats against the midnight chill, Hector caught me by the hand and led me back to the gallery.

'Good old Tommy and Sina,' I said, smiling. 'Always entertaining, even if they do seem to be only ever a step away from disaster. By the way, what did happen to Paul Taylor?'

Hector was silent for a moment. 'Let's save that story for another time. For now, I just want to enjoy the moment.'

'Suits me,' I replied, snuggling up to him. He was positively glowing after the exertion of ringing non-stop for half an hour.

He pointed to the still flickering candles before the altar. 'How many hundreds of villagers have started their New Years with this view?' he said softly. 'We are so lucky. Let's hope it's out best year yet, too, sweetheart.'

He turned towards me and took my face in his hands, pressing his lips gently to mine, perhaps more chaste and restrained than he might have been elsewhere.

'Oo-err! Does kissing someone in church mean you have to get married?' cried Sina from the doorway.

I pulled away from Hector, laughing.

'Not if you don't tell the vicar, Sina,' I replied. 'We'll keep your secret if you keep ours.'

'OK, but just remember I'd make a very good bridesmaid.'

Hector pulled the brim of her hat over her eyes to admonish her.

'We'll *bear* it in mind, Paddington.'

Sina groaned at his pun, before skipping happily down the stairs after her brother, wellies squeaking on the old stone steps, and out into the clear, frosty first night of a whole new year.

For More About Sophie Sayers and Friends

If you enjoyed Christmas with Sophie Sayers, please share your enthusiasm by leaving a review - or by buying paperback copies as Christmas presents for all your friends and relations!

***

To keep up to date in the New Year about all my stories, long and short, and other aspects of my writing life, please visit my website at www.authordebbieyoung.com and join my free Readers' Club. As a welcome gift, you'll also receive a free ebook of the novelette, The Pride of Peacocks, featuring Sophie and friends, and introducing St Bride's School.

***

My novels are published by Boldwood Books. If you'd like to receive their Debbie Young newsletter containing books news, competitions, and special offers, sign up at bit.ly/DebbieYoungNews.

Also by Debbie Young

All three series are still growing – and a new series will be launched in 2024.

***

Sophie Sayers Cozy Mysteries

Best Murder in Show

Murder at the Vicarage

Murder in the Manger

Murder at the Well

Springtime for Murder

Murder at the Mill

Murder Lost and Found

Murder in the Highlands

Driven to Murder (coming January 2024)

***

Gemma Lamb Cozy Mysteries

Dastardly Deeds at St Bride's

Sinister Stranger at St Bride's

Wicked Whispers at St Bride's

Artful Antics at St Bride's

***

Tales from Wendlebury Barrow Novelettes

The Natter of Knitters

The Clutch of Eggs

Milton Keynes UK
Ingram Content Group UK Ltd.
UKHW041814231123
433074UK00007B/3